Muriel's Reign

SUSANNA JOHNSTON is a former features writer for *Tatler*. Her books include *Five Rehearsals*, *Collecting*, *The Passionate Pastime*, *The Picnic Papers* (with co-editor Anne Tennant), *Parties: A Literary Companion* and *Muriel Pulls It Off*. She contributed to *The Englishwoman's House*, edited by Alvida Lees Milne, and she also edited *Late Youth: An Anthology Celebrating the Joys of Being Over Fifty*.

Muriel's Reign

SUSANNA JOHNSTON

Arcadia Books Ltd
15–16 Nassau Street
London W1W 7AB

www.arcadiabooks.co.uk

First published in the United Kingdom by Bliss Books, an imprint of Arcadia Books 2010
Copyright © Susannah Johnston 2010

A catalogue record for this book is available from the British Library.

ISBN 978-1-906413-56-9

Typeset in Garamond by MacGuru Ltd
Printed and bound in Finland by WS Bookwell

Arcadia Books gratefully acknowledges the financial support of Arts Council England.

Arcadia Books supports English PEN, the fellowship of writers who work together to promote
literature and its understanding. English PEN upholds writers' freedoms in Britain and around
the world, challenging political and cultural limits on free expression. To find out more, visit
www.englishpen.org or contact
English PEN, 6-8 Amwell Street, London ECIR IUQ

Arcadia Books distributors are as follows:

in the UK and elsewhere in Europe:
Turnaround Publishers Services
Unit 3, Olympia Trading Estate
Coburg Road
London N22 6TZ

in the US and Canada:
Independent Publishers Group
814 N. Franklin Street
Chicago, IL 60610

in Australia:
Tower Books
PO Box 213
Brookvale, NSW 2100

in New Zealand:
Addenda
PO Box 78224
Grey Lynn
Auckland

in South Africa:
Jacana Media (Pty) Ltd
PO Box 291784,
Melville 2109
Johannesburg

Arcadia Books is the *Sunday Times* Small Publisher of the Year 2002/03

Dedicated to both Stella Weatherall and George Christie with love and gratitude.

Chapter 1

The first thing that Muriel Cottle did after moving into Bradstow Manor was to go back on the promise she had made herself – that she would always use the pretty little bedroom that she had originally been allotted by a curmudgeonly servant on her first visit there.

Instead she moved into a large and airy one where she continued to cohabit with Peter, her blind brother-in-law and her dog, Monopoly.

After her inheritance she had played with the idea of changing her name but, since she hoped, eventually, to marry Peter, who was her husband's brother, there didn't appear to be any way out of being called 'Cottle' – a name she had never cared for.

Their courtship had been slow and comfortable and now, apart from the awkwardness of his being Hugh's brother, Peter kept her afloat – helped her to sail over the endless dilemmas that arose every day to cast shadows over the miracle of her fortune. On bad days she clung to him as to a plank in choppy water.

Many of her early days at Bradstow Manor had been

almost unendurable and there had been near-unanimous revolt amongst the underworked retainers.

Phyllis, the self-appointed housekeeper and one-time 'carer' to the former owner, showed scars of bitter betrayal beneath anaemic prettiness and dug even deeper than the rest.

'Of course. You never knew him. Never came to visit, did you? We all wondered what he got into his head when he willed the property over to you. But, then, he wasn't himself – and all those promises he made.'

Muriel had straightened her back in confidence – knowing she had no case to answer for. Since spending many hours with Jerome's solicitor, Arthur Stiller (labelled a 'sweetie' by the rector's wife), she understood more of the history of the place than she had done when first it had been thrust upon her.

'Phyllis. Once and for all. This house belonged to Mr Atkins's wife. My mother's cousin – Alice. She was descended from the family who actually built it and, as it turned out, Marco and I are the only leftovers of that line.'

She remembered the scene, wondering why she had described herself and Marco as 'leftovers', as she tidied a lampshade that was shedding threads.

Remembered, too, how in spite of the hurdles it promised, the first sighting of the house had set her heart beating with acquisitive desire.

She had not, though, consulted Arthur Stiller on the topic of divorcing Hugh. The solicitor, whose fingers looked like lardy dumplings, was too local, too much of a friend of the rector and his wife, to confide in on a matter where sensitivities were finely balanced.

Peter and Muriel had gingerly introduced the subject of divorce to Hugh who had favoured a hangdog expression and willed his face to turn a reddish shade.

'Frankly, both of you. I don't know what you're plotting. Is Muriel to cite me or am I to cite her – producing my own brother as co-respondent?'

'Oh Hugh,' Muriel had pleaded, 'can't we do it by post or something?'

'Come on, Muriel. I have my needs and, I might add, my rights. We were, still are, married when you came into – er – all this.'

Hugh knew – had heard from someone who had overheard – that an object of importance lay unexposed under the Elizabethan eaves. Muriel guessed that he guessed that she had something interesting to hide.

When, a month or so earlier, a thin young man and his fat secretary had arrived from London representing a firm of auctioneers, to value the contents of the house, it was possible that an amazing discovery had been made.

There was a small painting above the piano in the hall

that showed a chubby child holding up a bird. It looked very like a Bronzino hanging in the Uffizi and the thin young man, Muriel detected, wet his pants as he spotted it. He wore a grey flannel suit, checked shirt (so as not to look too formal in the country) and a smart tie. He carried a folder and held it in front of his trousers after the accident.

Muriel still waited to hear if the picture was, indeed, priceless.

Hugh suggested, 'Perhaps I could, at least, have a small painting? I always liked the one of the little boy holding up a bird. Reminds me (this he said tenderly) of Marco when he was small.'

They did not inch forward.

Before sleeping Muriel, in her mind, made a list of all members of her household – outlying ones and neighbours too.

Dulcie, more man than woman in the caravan with cats.

Sonia, ex-secretary and peculiar.

Kitty (angelic).

Extra daily helpers, mostly relations of Kitty.

Joyce and Eric (garden), both bad-tempered.

Phyllis, ex-carer to Jerome Atkins and a thorn in everybody's flesh.

Hugh, ex-husband in squash court.

Marco (son) and Flavia (daughter-in-law) with Cleopatra (small granddaughter) in old barn.

Dawson (rector) and his wife Delilah at the rectory.

Monopoly – her dog – once Hugh's.

On top of these, mixed and mingled in her consciousness, came extra members of a sprawling cast. Sporadic visitors. Queen Elizabeth (the Queen Mother), Mambles (Princess Matilda), Cunty and Farty (maids no longer of use at Buckingham Palace), and Moggan the Queen Mother's effeminate chauffeur. Lizzie, a clinging old schoolfriend. Dear David, an American writer.

These characters merged into one gruesome image as her head, touching Peter's, fell onto the luxurious pillow.

Chapter 2

Sonia, the pixilated secretary who had, during a period of many years, worked for Jerome Atkins, showed disapproval of the new regime; lady of the manor's husband living in the abandoned squash court whilst his brother slept in her bed.

She retired at once – leaving sheaves of fluttering, unfiled and incomprehensible papers in overflowing boxes in a dank and stuffy room at the back of the house; unpaid bills and sniffed-into paper handkerchiefs. On her departure she ordained that the 'office' was not to be dismantled and that she was to pop in daily to make sure that the cats were not abused.

Apart from Kitty, the celestial cook, Jerome's motley crowd of helpers had done nothing but obstruct Muriel's path since she first took possession of the house.

Muriel's inherited, lifelong friend, HRH Princess Matilda (younger by several years than her sister – the Monarch) had decreed that Hugh, disgraced MP, penniless, a womaniser and discarded husband, must be housed somewhere, however humble, on the estate.

Muriel's friendship with Matilda – known to her very few friends as Mambles – decided on by both sets of parents in the girls' infancies, was a thorn in Muriel's flesh but not, in spite of Mambles being a semi-drunken depressive, an intolerable one for she caused amusement and was affectionate in her way.

Muriel's immediate thought had been to convert the tack room for Hugh to live in. There were no horses at Bradstow – although two donkeys lived in a paddock alongside Dulcie; Dulcie was possibly a genuine hermaphrodite.

The tack room was small and she took pity – deciding to put her husband into a squash court that had been unused for at least fifty years.

It was bleak with light coming in mainly from the roof; walls tall and bare. Muriel, with unwelcome interference from Dulcie, had hung up threadbare carpets and installed a 'futon' on the gallery – smothering it in a duvet.

It was dreadfully uninviting and Hugh strove to make it more so – placing an ironing board in a prominent position and piling packets of 'meals for one' in spots where they could not fail to be noticed. He had decided to learn to play the flute and a music stand stood in one corner of the court. A couple of kitchen chairs were pulled up to a bare table on which perched, as reproachful reminder, a large photograph of his wedding to Muriel in which HRH Princess Matilda and Peter formed part of the group.

Then there was an empty dog basket to underline the unlikely possibility of Monopoly, originally his dog but now of altered allegiance, deserting Muriel at the big house and joining him in the squash court. Only the shower room shone; sparkling with vitamins, coloured mouthwash, cotton buds and battery-operated objects for dental care.

Moving him in had been ghastly. Mambles had suggested sending Cunty, a retired royal servant and now in Mambles's part-time employ, down to help and Muriel had considered turning her housekeeper, Phyllis, over to Hugh but feared he would sleep with her and cause confusion. He was hell bent on dismembering Muriel by thrusting guilt on her and often mentioned that he might become a trainee plumber or help in the garden from time to time.

He was beginning, with martyred enjoyment, to come to terms with his humiliation when Delilah, wife of the rector, called on him. The weather was cold and the sky already dark. Delilah carried a powerful torch that nearly blinded Hugh as he opened the door to her.

'Cooee. It's me. I've brought you a bottle of our home-brewed beer and want you to know that here, at Bradstow, we're very broadminded people. Dawson, my husband, is not judgemental – although he's rector, and says he believes that the extended family has Christian origins.'

Hugh asked her to sit on one of the kitchen chairs as she gazed at the wedding photograph. 'What a gorgeous picture. And HRH. She must have attended. Is that – er – your brother – the one acting as best man?'

She suggested that Hugh pay a visit to the rectory that very evening to eat mince pies and drink 'plonk'.

He said that he would like to; had no engagements and enjoyed a walk.

'Good. That's settled. We try to gather in a few lame dogs as Christmas draws near. It takes all sorts and we have a lovely parishioner coming to take pot-luck too this evening. He's a sweetie – but something, and this is very sad, went wrong with his chemistry and they say – well. Tittle-tattle. We're all God's creatures.'

Hugh walked quickly past the manor house – shuttered in a wintry way – and pictured, within, his wife in happy harmony with his brother beside a vast Elizabethan fireplace and Monopoly, his faithless dog, gloating in comfort as a Christmas to end all Christmases was planned. The entire village had been asked in to sing carols in the hall. His blind brother, acting as host, was to play the piano accompaniment and a suitably tall tree would be sure to stand in the well of the sturdy staircase.

He wondered as he neared the rectory if, over plonk and mince pies, he might be asked to help with the Sunday School or be roped in to 'beat the boundaries' on his wife's estate as he cleared his throat and waited to be greeted by an ecstatic Delilah.

'Our boy, Alastair, is here as luck would have it. And Tommy. Christian names only by the way. Rule of the village. We asked Dulcie to come along. She's lonely as well.'

Hugh was introduced to a subdued Alastair who, having been wooed by both daughters of some exiled member of the royal family thanks to an introduction from Muriel and Mambles, had escaped from the grasp of each – having failed to choose between them. They had both become anorexic and were at each other's throats after their separate rejections and Mambles remained in a state of high dudgeon against the rector's son. She had learnt 'through the back stairs' that Alastair had once been in trouble for dropping his trousers on public transport and refused to see why he couldn't have taken on both girls – 'time share or something'.

In Delilah's sitting room, Hugh was startled. Dulcie, his neighbour from the caravan, stared brutally at him from an oily rubber outfit that she had refused to remove in the hall, and said, 'Will you tell that wife of yours that there are some things that I cannot abide and incest is one of them. I gather that blind man she lives with happens to be your brother.'

Before Hugh had opened his mouth 'Tommy', fellow guest, interrupted with a wink and a giggle.

'Aren't you dishy. Tommy Tiddler. That's what they call me.' Just for a moment Hugh thought that he also said 'darling'.

Tommy Tiddler was fat, particularly round the middle, and wore an ermine stole, pinned on to one of his shoulders by a paste brooch in the shape of two goats committing, quite clearly, a sexual act. He reeked of scent that smelled as lemony as fluid used in public lavatories.

Dawson, in dog collar, joined them and asked, 'Might either of you two chaps be interested in helping with the Sunday School? Only three pupils at the moment. We could do with some fresh blood.'

Tommy Tiddler writhed and attempted to enthuse Hugh.

'One might enjoy,' he dimpled, 'take along a dressing-up box and some "bits". One's party trick is an imitation of the Queen Mum. Drape a quilt over the shoulder and pin it with this.' He touched the sexually intertwined goats.

Delilah wheeled round at the mention of the Queen Mother.

'Do you happen to know this, Hugh? Is there a chance of Muriel entertaining any "royals" over Christmas? I'll be decorating the church – gorgeous holly this year – and Dawson does a lovely sermon on Christmas Day. That is to say he does two. Midnight service of course on Christmas Eve. I'll need to know so as to keep pews free up near the front.'

Inwardly Hugh urged Delilah to ask him to read a lesson in church but had no luck. No point, mercifully, in her asking blind Peter. Perhaps Marco, his and Muriel's son, was to be chosen spokesman. Heir apparent.

Hugh knew nothing of Muriel's Christmas plans – other than that he was expected to lunch at the manor following the morning church service. Possibly on Boxing Day as well. Delilah was in full swing. 'Of course Christmas is a family occasion. We all envy you having that gorgeous little granddaughter. Of course you know Dulcie. She lives near you in the van and,' in a whisper, 'don't you pay too much attention to her rough manner. There are those who won't be served tea by her at the fete but I always say and Dawson agrees, she's a law unto herself … Now, Tommy. You'll be a comfort to each other. He may not look it but he's a churchgoer and a lonely soul like yourself.'

Tommy tried again with Hugh. 'One is a chef by trade. Nibbles and eats for special occasions. Let one know if ever one's entertaining.' Hugh thought of his solitary meal unfreezing as Tommy Tiddler spoke.

Then, getting closer so that scented fumes flew up Hugh's nostrils, Tommy pointed in the direction of Alastair who gangled in the corner of the room.

'Of course you know of his disgrace. Would that one had witnessed.'

Hugh stepped backwards. Did Delilah really intend that he make friends with this fright left over from the fifties? Cross dress with him at Sunday School?

He had, after all, knocked around a bit and wondered if this relic of post-war England was symptomatic of small village life.

He strode back through Muriel's kingdom, dejected, cold and at sea, towards the bachelor minginess of the old squash court.

The degree to which he had already been degraded curdled his blood. Returning, as he had, from Johannesburg to find his wife not only having landed a magnificent place but having installed his inadequate brother, Peter, within it.

Since earliest days he had considered his brother to be weird and a drip – despising his aspiration to become a poet and his mannerly ways.

Now what?

Peter had triumphed over him. Cornered a comfortable study; slept with Muriel and had kidnapped his dog.

He, Hugh, made do in an outhouse. It was all intolerable.

However, as he heated up a 'meal for one', he allowed himself to think that Muriel's housekeeper, Phyllis, was not unattractive.

Chapter 3

Phyllis had been washed up; more often than not on sharp, litter-strewn beaches. Her mother, a single parent from a small Welsh town, had instilled in her the fact that her face was to be her fortune.

Nothing else was likely to provide her with one.

She left school early and took odd jobs but none of them brought her fortune. Events led her from rented rooms to factory work, to other towns, to occasional adventures but nothing rose to the standard of the early promises made by her mother.

Fred was the nearest she got. He was handsome and a sporadic big spender; rode a motorcycle and rented a furnished basement flat near Central London.

He worked, he told her, for J. Arthur Rank and rewarded her with descriptions of the cinema trade as they ate in restaurants. Phyllis settled for it. Her higher expectations had dwindled and she took a morning job cleaning for a family who were good to her and was grudgingly contented.

One afternoon Fred was knocked off his motorbike

as he drove the wrong way down a one-way street. He died in the ambulance as it made its way to the nearest hospital. Phyllis was saddened for she had liked Fred well enough and was anxious about her future.

J. Arthur Rank's were, obviously, excellent employers but unlikely to know much about pensions for common-law wives.

The day after Fred's death she looked up the firm in the telephone book. Fred had never allowed her to ring him at work.

'Always up a ladder fixing a bit of lighting. In and out, I am, like a fiddler's elbow.'

A lady at the office number listed for Rank Productions said, 'No.' No Mr Reardly had ever worked there as far as she knew. She would check, of course, but felt there must be some mistake. 'Another firm, dear, called Rank, I daresay. There are plenty of them. The fur trade perhaps?'

Phyllis was never able to track down Fred's past. Never, entirely, did she find out how he had passed his days or where he had found inspiration for the stories he cooked up for her about the film industry as they ate out.

For a short while she continued with the cleaning job but soon the flat was reclaimed by an angry landlord who tried to make Phyllis pay back rent as Fred's few possessions were confiscated and his employment as burglar hinted at.

A live-in job was her only hope and it was with that only hope that she read the lines in a domestic journal: 'Carer needed for elderly gentleman. Nursing experience not essential.'

The advertisement took her to Lincolnshire where Jerome Atkins lived and where his mind had started to judder.

Arthur Stiller, solicitor, had interviewed her and deemed her suitable. He liked a pretty face and Phyllis's was prettier than any of the other applicants.

He said, 'Bear with me,' as he left her on a chair in his office – 'I must have a little think.' He had already decided to offer her the post.

She stretched her eyes when she was shown the vast house and stretched them further when she was shown to an attic room, roses papered on walls and ceiling, and told it was where she was to make her home. Old furniture too – and oil paintings. It was not hers – but surely a fortune lurked.

Other members of the household were hostile and the outdoor staff disdainful but it suited her in several ways.

Her first meeting with Jerome Atkins, her new employer, was encouraging. His wife was alive but only just and lived in seclusion in a cut-off wing of the place with her own team of helpers.

He looked younger than his eighty-four years, had

a good head of white hair, winged eyebrows and tight, hard, unwrinkled skin.

Mrs Atkins died soon after Phyllis's arrival. Her husband was little affected by the event but enjoyed Phyllis decking him out for the funeral service, conducted by Dawson in the village church. She brushed his collar, polished his shoes and tucked a handkerchief into the pocket of his dark suit.

Nothing she did inched her nearer to extracting promises from him although, as he grew daily pottier, he enjoyed telling her of his astonishing wealth. 'Me. Me. Very rich, you know. Oh yes. Very rich indeed. You — like some?'

Phyllis would have loved some but never knew when to strike or even whether or not the iron was hot. She had no knack.

'Write down,' he insisted. 'Write it down. Write down what you want.' But it was not for her to do the writing. Once he did hint that he had asked Arthur Stiller to draft something in her favour but she was never able to find out more about it.

He became ever more taunting and unpleasant and she performed her tasks with less enthusiasm — allowing his clothes to become rank and his shoes scuffed.

Several years had passed and Phyllis had become a part, albeit a lazy and discontented one, of the household and, with the possibility of Jerome 'doing something for her' nothing better had cropped up.

Then the blow. As Jerome's mental powers deteriorated, this flipping Muriel had been sent for. Heiress as it turned out. Jerome had mentioned a 'niece' occasionally but never with conviction.

Phyllis searched for any form of concealed codicil but nothing showed. Nothing promised. Nothing but loneliness and insecurity. Even her mother had died. She didn't know if her auntie still lived in the small town in Wales where she had spent her childhood.

Chapter 4

Muriel, comparing the date with her first terrifying Christmas as owner of Bradstow Manor, was very nearly contented. It was excellent to have Peter to help in all matters. What was not so good but indeed a horrible hindrance, a constant embarrassment and nagging reminder of dire days, was to have Hugh living in barely suppressed fury in the squash court.

Muriel had fallen in love with Peter, gradually but passionately, during the years of her husband's infidelities and had, after many a complication, become his lover and constant companion.

Peter had braved himself to allow for the unorthodoxy of the circumstances and to rise above the dilemma relating to his personal footing in the house.

Being blind – he fancied himself, too, to be invisible. He doted on Muriel and was assured of the inexorability of the reinforcement that he provided for her. He lived in accord with a strange compensatory law that allowed him to enjoy what was on offer.

Hugh had always, since childhood, been foul to him

– condescending and prickly. Foul, too, in Peter's view, to Muriel – subjecting her to humiliation and contempt, grotesquely underestimating her magnificence.

Peter planned to lie low. After all he cost nothing. Hugh could never charge him with venality. Even after waiving the rent from his London house in order to provide his futile nephew with an income, he was able to support his own modesty of financial need. Neither Hugh nor Marco had a case of that nature for him to answer. He was tremendously happy.

Muriel had lived in the house for over a year but didn't count the Christmas gone by as a true one for she had been beset with problems that lacked pattern.

She'd had no idea, then, who was supposed to drag in the tree; where it was normally placed or if, indeed, there had ever been a tree in the house at Christmas.

This year she was more organised in her crowded brain but sincerely wished that Mambles wasn't coming and bringing 'Mummy', Cunty, Farty and Moggan the driver.

Then there was the problem of her son Marco, her daughter-in-law Flavia and Cleopatra the baby – nearly a year old and badly behaved. They lived in a converted barn – also organised for them by Muriel in bossy association with Mambles. The trouble was that she had difficulty in persuading the young family to use it.

'No one to babysit, Ma, and Flavia's hopeless at

house-running,' Marco often told her as he dumped a furious Cleopatra on the floor of the kitchen and bounded with Flavia to one of Muriel's comfortable spare rooms.

Mambles and her mother intended to stay for an indefinite number of nights but refused to say how many.

'It's awful at Windsor now,' Mambles had yawned down the telephone. 'Not like it was when the King was alive. Fergie plays tiresome practical jokes and Diana won't eat anything. Mummy's had enough.'

The worst problem for Muriel was finding extra men. Mambles loathed being placed next to women at meals. She was certain to encourage Hugh who flirted with her and she couldn't stand Peter who had no inkling of how to flirt.

Some weeks earlier she had persuaded her old and dear American friend David, to join them. He, in his own words, 'went for anything that was on offer,' and had accepted with amused delight. Then, only two evenings before, had telephoned to say that he was unwell and must stay at home in his solitary London flat.

Maybe that peculiar Tommy Tiddler, who rented the old school building and who wore shawls and wobbled when he moved, would come in handy.

There was, too, a judge, a widower, who lived nearby and who had angled for over a year to be invited by

Muriel to share in her good fortune. He had been disqualified from his profession for goosing a member of the jury but, Delilah insisted, 'It was no more than a prank.'

Muriel had kept a letter from him, a few weeks' old and unanswered; had thrown it into a basket where it lay near the top of a pile of incoming post. The basket was at her feet beside Monopoly and the fire. She leant to ask Peter for advice on how to handle each letter in turn as Hugh trudged past the house in melancholy puzzlement on his way to the squash court after the rectory party.

The judge's letter was alive with screech marks and read:

'Hail once again to my new neighbour! I know you have been busy. I'm constantly hearing of great doings under the new regime! Great tidings that Bradstow Manor has been handed down through family connections! Too many jumped-up Johnnie's in this neighbourhood! Last thing we want are any more estate agents.'

He told her, too, that he owned an interesting house not far from hers; that his 'lady wife' had died seven years earlier and that he hoped they could meet up. (Meet with Muriel – not with his wife.)

Peter suggested inviting him to lunch on Boxing Day and Muriel wished she knew if he had been knighted before goosing the member of the jury. Wasn't sure how to address him.

Then there was the problem of church services. Mambles was certain to duck them but her mother, still aware of having been consort to a King Emperor, liked ceremony.

Village jammed with detectives. Crackers. Dogs. The royal dogs, Jubilee and Sir Walter Raleigh, upsetting Monopoly and causing havoc in Dulcie's cat kingdom.

Her old schoolfriend, Lizzie, also had to be included. Lizzie had altered in behaviour since first hearing of Muriel's unexpected inheritance. At that juncture she had been brittle and undermining. 'What a foul thing to happen. I'd loathe to have to live in the country. Especially Lincolnshire.'

A year later she chose other tactics. Poor relation tactics. 'You are lucky. You have your live-in lover in your bed, your husband in the squash court and your son in the barn. Living alone on a budget, as I do, is a very different thing.'

'I know I'm lucky,' Muriel answered as her head burst with anxious thoughts.

Lizzie didn't much like Muriel; found her earthy and dowdily dressed but was, nonetheless, unstoppable in her demands.

In Lizzie's view Muriel was scatty and uninterested in art exhibitions or jewellery – even in clothes – but seemed to attract one drama after another and there was always a fear of missing out on excitement if she didn't keep in constant contact by inviting herself, mercilessly, to stay.

Muriel found Lizzie unstoppable in her deadly liveliness.

She walked, past treasures, to the kitchen that had been improved and re-stocked since she moved in, and found Kitty preparing brandy butter to store away for Christmas Day. She ladled a large quantity of brandy, hinting that she was beginning to get familiar with the tastes of Queen Elizabeth and her daughter. Muriel asked if she knew whether or not the local judge had been knighted.

'No. Poor soul. The disgrace came too soon for that. Killed his wife, they say. Not so much the disgrace as the failure to get a decoration.'

Back in the sitting room where Peter and Monopoly talked to each other, Muriel wrote a card to the judge and to Tommy Tiddler – addressing them both correctly. Tommy's surname was, in fact, Trout.

She went to bed earlier than Peter. Monopoly always waited for him and it was a marvel how they never faltered in finding their way through the confusing house.

The bedroom was uncluttered. Little for Peter to knock against. It was large and comfortable and she loved it. Loved everything except for Christmas, what it entailed, Hugh and Phyllis and the outdoor helpers.

She did think that she loved Cleopatra in the way that she knew she ought but found her hindering and understood, as she had understood when Hugh first left her in charge of his dog, that much of her lack of enthusiasm was Marco and Flavia's fault for dumping the baby on her at problematic moments. They were responsible for her lack of grandmotherly affection. She hoped she might enjoy Cleopatra more when she became a toddler. Muriel loved the word 'toddler'.

Also she had anxious doubts about Cleopatra's paternity. Wondered whether she was, biologically, her grandmother at all. Flavia had wandered early in her marriage to Marco. Had taken up with a bounder. Possibly several.

Chapter 5

Muriel woke early and, after letting Monopoly into the garden, walked again to the kitchen. It was exactly eight-thirty but to her dismay she found Hugh, wearing faded corduroy trousers and a butcher's apron, holding a teapot in one hand and a wire wool contraption in the other. He looked concerned.

'Never seen a dirtier teapot, Muriel,' he said as he scoured, 'I thought I'd make myself useful and introduce a bit of hygiene into your domain.'

She was sorry that Monopoly was in the garden. He might have bitten Hugh.

'Another thing, Muriel,' Hugh gathered confidence, 'those antibiotics I found by the toaster. I've thrown them away. Dreadful things. I didn't want Cleopatra to swallow them.'

'Hugh. They're mine. I've had bronchitis. I have to finish the course.'

It was impossible to tell Hugh that he was not wanted in the house. They were still married. For all she knew he might be part owner although old Jerome Atkins had left it solely to her.

It crossed her mind that Lizzie might ignite Hugh over Christmas. She had suspected that they had been up to no good together during an inharmonious patch of her marriage. There was a chance of her returning to the scene as one wallowing in an old cardigan; nestling under the duvet on the futon in the squash court during holiday festivities.

'That teapot,' she said, 'is very old and very fragile. Please stop attacking it.'

As her voice hardened Phyllis came in through the back door. She looked pleased as punch and her petticoat buzzed.

Hugh turned to her and said, 'Doing a bit of your dirty work, Phyllis.'

'It's not my job. I'm housekeeper – not maid of all work, Mr Cottle.' She called Hugh 'Mr Cottle' and Peter 'Peter'.

Hugh looked at her with lechery and his eyes watered at her appearance but he was quickly distracted for Marco burst in; early for him. 'We didn't get a wink last night. Flav's had it. So have I.'

Cleopatra, gripped in Marco's arms, had been crying but stopped and stretched her arms towards Muriel who had a thousand things to do and needed no delays that morning. She took the heavy baby from her son who drew away and said, 'Thanks, Ma. I'm going to join Flav for a shut-eye.'

Cleopatra was hot, wet and floppy and Muriel felt resentful and frantic. She sat the baby on the kitchen table and looked at her as she planned the next move. Cleopatra stared back – cool blue eyes – tremendously like Hugh's. This realisation was mixed as a blessing, if Cleopatra amounted to such, but, if well nurtured might end up as one. The stare more or less established in Muriel's eyes Cleopatra's paternity and, after all, Peter – although a total opposite in character and manner – did look, feature by feature, very like Hugh. Peter's influence must come to bear.

So. Hugh was in all probability Cleopatra's grandfather and might be handy as a childminder – but something held Muriel back. She wanted nothing to belong jointly to Hugh and herself – not even a grandchild, even if he came in handy. Too underlining.

Marco bounded off as Phyllis showed delight to see Muriel at a disadvantage again and as Hugh said, 'Ahem, Muriel. Not my department as you know. You've always had a knack with the little ones.'

Cleopatra was teething and fretful; showing a red blob on one cheek.

Hugh suggested, 'Can't they get an au pair – a Filipino or something?' Hugh was always ready with long-term solutions but never solved a problem on the spot.

Muriel, desperate, electric with tension and tired by fighting panic, held tight to the hot baby.

Once again she told Hugh to stop scouring the teapot whatever else and suggested that he go back to the squash court.

'Not wanted I see, Muriel,' – tenderly and with eyes again watery. 'We were happy together, weren't we?'

'No, Hugh. Never. Never and certainly not now. Buzz off.' She said 'Buzz off' twice – near to losing control. The buzz of Phyllis's petticoat had reminded her of the sound of the word.

Placing Cleopatra on the table but keeping an arm around her, with her free hand she pulled a box towards her. Looking into it, she saw two pots of plum jam with shiny transparent paper covering them and banded with elastic. Two pots of honey too. Honey was provided for the house by the unprepossessing Joyce who kept her bees by the greenhouse.

Phyllis watched with deadly eyes.

'Mr Cottle. Mr Cottle, your husband – not the other one – forgot to take these. I set them aside for him. It's miserable – what he has to make do with.'

Muriel seethed. Hugh had been allocated the reasonable rent collected from her London house. Marco and Flavia were given the rent from Peter's. Both houses were let to young couples who searched to buy their own. Each separate dependant, Hugh and Marco, had, with care, the opportunity to be self-sufficient.

Cleopatra shunted towards the box and tried to pierce the cellophane with wet fingers.

'Our households, Phyllis, are supposed to be separate.'

'Seems a shame,' she muttered as she wrenched the parcel from Cleopatra and whirled away with it.

Muriel, with two biscuits in her pocket and Cleopatra in her arms, walked to the study where Peter wrote verse and where a playpen lived; ready for emergency use.

Cleopatra, almost immediately, fell asleep; both biscuits wet and crumbling in her hands.

Muriel sat beside Peter, told him of events, of the scouring, of Cleopatra's resemblance to Hugh and read the messages on Christmas cards aloud to him. In the main they came from neighbours – angling for an invitation to Bradstow Manor in the New Year.

'Muriel,' Peter said. 'There's no point whatsoever in any of this unless you learn to enjoy it – after all I am here to help you.'

She softened and was tranquilised.

The telephone rang on Peter's desk and Muriel answered it. It was Delilah.

'Muriel! Getting ready for Christmas! Such a busy time. We are all envious of you. I know that envy is a sin but we do envy you your lovely Christmas with your gorgeous little granddaughter. One more thing. Might any of your – er, visitors be in church over the festivities?'

As Cleopatra, wearing creased pyjamas that nearly burst with heavy nappies, slept on the boards of the playpen, Muriel opened more and more cards.

Chapter 6

Leaving Cleopatra asleep in Peter's study and wishing that grandmotherly sentiments hadn't eluded her, Muriel went to the front door to find Monopoly. She always experienced the same fear when she did this; the fear that Monopoly, on an unexplained whim, might have gone to the squash court in search of Hugh, his old master.

Monopoly, however, bounded towards her and she dismissed the perfect image in her mind of a smiling granddaughter in a party frock, placed before her by doting parents who raced to reclaim her.

As she let the dog in she spied a fellow on a motor-bike whizzing down the drive and knew, too late, that he had pinched the money left out as Christmas box for the paper boy. She had drawn a bit of holly on the corner of the envelope.

There was much to think about. Phyllis took an age to return from delivering Hugh's parcel of jam and honey even if, earlier, she had complained of being run off her feet.

Muriel wasn't yet certain as to where Phyllis's duties lay. She knew she opened and closed the shutters morning and evening, waved her arms about and talked of preparing rooms – although there were other, younger, girls who did the donkey work.

She was disappointed that her good American friend, David, had been unable to come for Christmas too. She had invited him, knowing it to be a risk, since his conversation was often unedited and louche. Nonetheless he was lively, she was devoted to him and he had pronounced her new life – the house – her domestic arrangement with Peter and everything connected with it – to be sensational. At the start he had accepted to come but later telephoned to say he was unwell and that he was writing to explain himself.

Muriel had spotted an old navy blue pram in the tack room. It was set on high springs and was double-ended with a well in the middle. She prayed that there would never be need for more than one of the ends. The fabric in the hoods was tattered but it was something to pop Cleopatra into. Marco and Flavia hadn't invested in anything useful and Muriel knew that, soon, she must find a solution but knew nothing of local shops for perambulators. She wanted Phyllis to sort it out. Immediately.

Phyllis did reappear as Joyce and Eric, both furious, lurched into the hall with a vast Christmas tree and wanted to know where it was to be placed.

Flushed and gesticulating, Phyllis said, 'Stopped to

give Mr Cottle a bit of a tidy and he made me a cup of coffee. Nescafe, that is to say.'

'I want that old pram in the tack room to be cleaned up and we must see to the rooms.'

As she spoke she hoped that Cleopatra was still unconscious in Peter's study.

Phyllis ignored the request to restore the pram but brightened at the talk of rooms. Rooms for royalty. The Queen Mother, Princess Matilda, Cunty and Farty. Moggan in the attic up amongst antlers and Phyllis. There was no danger there concerning Phyllis for Moggan was 'not the marrying kind'.

'Will it be two chamber pots? I know the Princess has need of one but what about her mother?'

Muriel guessed that Queen Elizabeth wore padding but said, 'No. One. One will be enough.'

It was exciting in the bedrooms. They started with that of Queen Elizabeth. A small fridge had been delivered, put in a corner of the room and stacked with liquid refreshment for both her and the Princess. Cunty's room was next door and Muriel asked Phyllis to find a bucket with a lid on it; requested by Cunty for the padding. Muriel didn't enlarge on its use. They made sure that the chamber pot, decorated in roses, was near the bed in Mambles's room. That was one thing that Mambles flatly refused to do – to travel on foot during the night.

Their stay was not necessarily to be a long one although they never told in advance of the exact number of days they planned on. Cut winter flowers were unlikely to survive for more than a few hours with the heating turned up high so pot plants, furnished with weird water-dribbling contraptions recommended by Dulcie, flourished in both rooms. Dulcie had read of these odd objects in one of her weekly editions of *Fur and Feathers* although they were actually intended to water baby chicks.

When everything was regally prepared Muriel and Phyllis returned to the hall – Muriel pausing to listen at Peter's study door where all was silent and remembering to mention to anyone concerned that Farty was unable to drink any milk other than goat's.

She returned to the subject of the pram and Phyllis, with rotten grace, replied, 'All right then. It's in shreds. Seems a shame. You'd have thought …'

Lizzie's room was ready too. Muriel strained to add touches equal to those of Mambles and her mother (barring chamber pot) for fear of Lizzie's comparisons. She was certain to snoop upon arriving, as she was due to do, before the others. She had already telephoned three times that morning – twice about the time of her train arrival and once about clothes – 'What sort of evening dresses should I bring to keep my end up with your smart friends?'

Muriel was planning her next move when Flavia crept up on her; startlingly dressed and carrying a tin of baby food and a bottle.

'I've had a squizz in the study and Peter's doing fine. Cleopatra's still asleep. I knew she wouldn't be any trouble. Be a chick and give her these when she wakes up. Me and Marco are off to join Tommy Tiddler at the pub. Good old Gran.'

Flavia, Muriel noticed, had started to take a morbid interest in clothes. Her outfits had become showier and more expensive-looking as though to prove that, in spite of living in a barn in her mother-in-law's garden and of having produced a baby, she could still hold her own in a more sophisticated world; that she had in no way been diminished by country air. Clothes were transformed into armour.

Lizzie was likely to sense competition and to stiffen at being sartorially outdone – even by one many years her junior.

Muriel had no idea what to do. She was near to trembling and cross. She took the tin and the bottle and said, 'Okay, Flav, but come straight back and take her for a walk. I'm having an old pram cleaned and I'll get you a new one after Christmas.'

'Straight back? We'll probably have a bit of fodder while we're there.'

She pirouetted elegantly and ran off saying, 'Can't wait. Marco's hooting his horn.'

Muriel screamed, 'I'll push her round at three o'clock.'

'Don't worry. We'll fetch her when we're through.'

When Muriel went to Peter's study Cleopatra was writhing; ready to wake and livid. She lifted the smelly child from the pen, glared at the tins of baby food left by Flavia and looked at her watch. It was only midday.

Kitty, the angelic cook, knocked on the door.

'You can't go feeding her that, Mrs Cottle. I'll mash her up some chicken and potato – and greens when you and Mr Peter have your lunch. I've got Gemma and Lara with me this morning in the kitchen. We'll take her over to the barn and get her cleaned up – and dressed. They always leave the door ajar.'

When Muriel had put another note into another envelope and drawn another bit of holly and placed it on the door handle, she realised that the paper boy had already called and left empty-handed.

She and Peter went to the small table in the dining-room window and found that Kitty had wedged an old wooden high chair between the places where they were to sit. Kitty reappeared followed by thrilled Gemma and Lara – hair in Kirby grips, carrying a glowing Cleopatra. It hit her. The sensation she had yearned for. A grandmotherly glow as Cleopatra gave her a heavenly smile. Kitty said, 'It took a while to get her scrubbed up. Gemma found the frock; still in its wrapping since you brought it back from London.'

Cleopatra ate some of the chicken and vegetables and threw some around the room; spattering silver and glass. Muriel's grandmotherly glow lasted less than an hour after which she began to long for Marco and Flavia's return and resolved to be firm.

Lizzie was due to arrive in the evening and doubtless expected her quarters to match the comforts of other visitors; barring chamber pots, lidded buckets and alcohol. She told Muriel, earlier by telephone, 'Don't worry a scrap about me in your grand house with your grand guests.' Muriel loathed the word 'grand'.

'I'll have a very heavy suitcase. Masses of clothes, of course. As you know the only thing I can't stand is cold. I get physically ill when I'm cold. Actually sick.'

No sign of Marco or Flavia and Muriel became frantic. She swallowed her prejudices and decided to dump the baby on Hugh; playpen too.

Cleopatra, even when writhing and flailing, was transportable in Muriel's arms – across the yard and down a path to the squash court although it was windy and wet. The playpen, she decided, must be delivered later and left forever in Hugh's charge.

Eric and Joyce, her main and disliked outdoor helpers,

claimed to be occupied with wreaths and holly – worthy of a Queen or, at any rate, her mother. Later they must be urged to move the pen. She wrapped a woolly coat round Cleopatra. Kitty had fished it out from the muddle in the barn for Flavia had delivered her coatless.

Hugh was practising the flute when Muriel and Cleopatra charged in without knocking. Not far from where he stood in front of the music stand, a game of patience was laid out on a card table – sighing signal of solitude. Muriel was fairly certain that the game had not progressed since the last time she had popped in with a wastepaper basket.

'Goodness me, Muriel.' He cleared his throat and put the flute to one side. 'What a pleasant event. A visit from you and our lovely granddaughter.' He spoke in a voice of reverence and looked tenderly at them as he encouraged his eyes to brim. 'Next time perhaps you could bring Monopoly.'

Muriel, desperate to leave them to it and to get on with preparations, said, 'I can only stop for a moment Hugh but I hope you will be able to look after Cleopatra until Marco and Flavia get back from a jaunt to the pub.'

Hugh, thunderstruck, decided to take his chance, to stake his claim, to show grandparental responsibility and involvement.

'Of course. Come little one. I'll teach her to play the flute and, er, bond.'

Filled with doubts and some regrets, Muriel fled to the warmth of Peter's study and related all to his amusement. She was relieved that they were close and together as they discussed the forlorn enterprise of entertaining – the dimness and uncertainty involved in aiming to be hospitable. She felt, she told Peter, that her past was never to be over and that their future together was shapeless. Peter was having none of it and explained, very patiently and to her satisfaction, that they were happy. She knelt beside him and he held his hand heavily on her head. She liked the weight of it.

Chapter 7

An extra Christmas post had brought a letter from her friend David explaining in more detail his last-minute refusal to be with them all.

'Darling Muriel. I had bought gifts for everyone, very special gifts, but, oh, I so regret I shan't be able to give them round, all of you gathered about what I imagine, in the full fantastic flush of my imagination, a Christmas tree in the grand hall rising to the high Elizabethan beams, scintillating with gaudy ornaments and twinkling lights. And then Christmas luncheon in the dining room with its wainscoting so attractively warped with age, the great roasted turkey served on a massive serving dish (in America, platter, an old English word preserved in the still devoted ex-colony) surrounded by holly and mistletoe. HRH delighting in eating a whole leg? Up the ancient wooden stairs, the treads at picturesque angles and the newel posts worn from centuries of palsied hands clutching at them for support. I could go on and on, and do in fantasy, a fantasy I so wish I could realise in fact, but, my darling Muriel, I am not well, not at all well, with, I think, the Spanish flu, perhaps the very, very last in the world to suffer from that epidemic, once thought eradicated, but caught by me in a rather louche way in a rather remote part of the world, where the Spanish flu is said to have come back among the young attractive natives.

You are wonderfully aware of how much your invitations mean to me, I, an American trying to learn the ways of the British, which passport I am so proud to say I have been honoured with – though I must say I am puzzled, for my passport identifies me as a British citizen, not a subject. Has the United Kingdom become a republic without the royals knowing?'

She was sorry about the Spanish flu and not to be seeing him. David did so appreciate the marvels of the house. Few of her visitors or dependants appeared to have noticed anything very special about it although Peter, with high enthusiasm, often made her describe every cranny to him in detail.

Flavia, followed by an unsteady Marco, floundered into the hall where the Christmas tree had been installed and where piles of cut holly lay on plastic sheeting ready to decorate pictures and clocks. It was clear to Muriel as she walked down the stairs, having again checked on Lizzie's bedroom, that both Marco and Flavia were very drunk. She wondered which of the two had driven the car back from the pub.

'Hi Ma,' Marco, wearing a fixed grin, held tight to the stair rail as he waited for his mother to reach the bottom step. 'Getting ready for royalty? Is your show on the road?'

They both smoked cigarettes and seemed anxious to cover tracks; to divert attention from their absenteeism.

'Great fodder at The Bell. That Tommy Tiddler is a scream. Had us all in fits. I had to warn him not to do his imitation of the Queen Mother on Boxing Day as she'll be here in person. He thought I was kidding.'

He lurched and Flavia took over. 'Where's Cleopatra? Can you be a chick and continue the love-in with your granddaughter a bit longer? We need a nap. Touch of flu.'

They both teetered.

Muriel told them that they would find their small daughter learning to play the flute with her grandfather in the squash court and advised them to fetch her on their way home.

Marco smiled stupidly and said, 'Steady on, Ma. We need a bit of shut-eye. Good on you, though, for sharing grandparental responsibility with Pa.'

Muriel objected to the word 'responsibility' and rage mounted as she begged her son, beloved but confusing, and his pretty, dressy, drunk and feckless wife to retrieve their child.

Phyllis, who loved tinsel, began to decorate the tree. Outside it was wet and windy and darkness settled early. Muriel fretted that the heating was not turned up to the right temperature and wished she understood the system – reluctant to ask advice from anyone about anything.

She turned to the handsome staircase. Worth checking just once more on Lizzie's room. As she trod on the third step there was a soft click and the electricity went off. Only dim light, losing force by the second, came from various windows. The house had lately been rewired and she was indignant. Peter, who had heard her exclaim, called her.

'Come in here, Muriel, before it gets dark. My study. There's a good fire banked up. We can do a bit of chatting as we wait for developments. Lizzie will make a meal of it. I daresay the telephone's off too by the way and radiators will soon start to cool.'

There had been a strong wind and Peter guessed that a fallen tree had dislocated not only the lights but also the telephone.

She joined him and wondered about the Aga and if it was fired electrically. Water too. Did Kitty, for instance, have any backup in the kitchen? She was not due to come in until later. What of the squash court? Hugh floundering with the flute and the baby. No way, presumably, of heating up his 'dinner for one'.

Peter was musing. 'Too late to put them off I fear. They'll have to lump it. Might do them good – not that we want Mummy to croak from hypothermia and cause a scene.'

'Peter. Please. And Lizzie. Christ!'

The house was getting colder and Lizzie's train had already left a London station. No television either and Lizzie withered without a diet of 'soaps'.

Muriel suddenly noticed that a foul and continuous wail came from somewhere near the front door. A shrill bleep. Peter said, 'That'll be the burglar alarm.' One had recently been installed. 'I think we'll have to put up with that noise until the power comes back or, at any rate, until the battery gives out.'

A purse-lipped Phyllis came in carrying two candles and with a torch tucked under one arm. She was followed by Dulcie who was wrapped in vast outer garments, and in a towering rage. She charged into the study and shouted against the noise of the alarm. 'Two trees down. Goodness only knows when they will be seen to. Lines will be jammed I daresay. Not that we can phone from here. And you'd better unplug that Braille machine of yours.' She glared at Peter who saw nothing. 'It'll explode when the lights come on again – that is if they do this side of Christmas.'

Her bifocals glittered in the firelight as she prepared to

plunge further. 'I've got gas in the van so the cats are all right. That is to say that Corin, my Burmese, is suffering from asthma. Other than that someone's been bloody stupid. Fancy not getting that old generator repaired when they did all those fancy bits round here. I once worked in an architects' (she pronounced the word as it was spelled) office and I know what bloody idiots they all are – including that damned imbecile you had to help, if that's the word, with your alterations. I will not say "improvements".'

Dulcie had worn herself out and sat glowering on an armchair as daylight faded.

Joyce had been detailed to fetch Lizzie from the station and Muriel began to get nervy, apprehensive and infuriated. The wail from the alarm continued as she floundered in a hinterland of unwanted consequences.

Chapter 8

At last the burglar alarm stopped. The emergency batteries had died out and the hall was still warm when Lizzie, in thick fur, arrived, although the tree stood black and gloomy having lost its fairy lights.

The fire raged and candles branched from all angles.

Dulcie had staggered in, swearing, with long-abandoned Tilley Lamps so that Lizzie, on arriving, failed to notice anything untoward. Modest, now, she embraced Muriel.

'Lovely and warm. You know how I mind.'

She sighed as Muriel wished that Hugh, Marco or Flavia might be useful instead of multiplying her complications – loathing her own vacillating ways when it came to any one of them.

'So lovely to be here,' said Lizzie. 'My presents are in the bag. Rather modest I'm afraid. Shall I put them under the tree? I couldn't think what to bring for the royals so I got them chocolates. Expensive ones, I might add. No lights!'

No sooner had Lizzie noticed the lack of fairy lights than Delilah almost swam into the house.

'Cooee! Just to check you are all right. There's a tree down in the field and another across the road. No one knows when the power will be back or the telephone. I've left Dawson in the dark but, as you know, he's an academic and is content to be alone with his thoughts – and a torch.'

Muriel, after more than a year in the house, still uncertain as to who had produced the candles, lit the fires or generally administered, said, 'We're fine. Thank you very much.'

'You must introduce me to your visitor and, er, have any of the others arrived yet? Dulcie let slip that royalty might be expected. Will any of them be attending the church service?'

Lizzie, no longer reverent, was on the job.

'No heating? I'm sorry. I'll be ill. What a nuisance I am. When did it go out? You might have warned me. I'll survive I suppose but what about the Queen Mother? She's over ninety.'

As if Muriel didn't know. She willed Lizzie not to go on but said, 'I'm sorry, Lizzie. It's only just happened. Someone's finding out. It's sure to come on again before long.'

Kitty joined the group. 'I've got a Bunsen burner in the kitchen and bottled water.'

'Can I fill a hot-water bottle?' Lizzie's voice began to get louder.

Delilah departed without any information.

Together, with a hot-water bottle filled to lukewarm from a cooling kettle, Muriel and Lizzie passed through candlelit passages to Lizzie's room which was also bright with night lights, candles – even an old oil lantern as Muriel marvelled at the amazing competence of these emergency arrangements. The radiators, however, were already no more than tepid.

Lizzie asked, twice, how long it was to be before the power came back.

Promising to return, Muriel left Lizzie in her room and hoped that the groups from the outhouses managed independently. She dreaded Cleopatra clutching at candles or Hugh masquerading as invaluable during troubled times.

Worse still – what if they elected to move in with her and her Tilley Lamps until problems were solved?

When she sat down beside Peter he told her that Kitty had been to see him; to say that the house was swarming with her sisters and sisters-in-law and that Phyllis had bolted to the squash court with candles, provisions and a bottle of Château d'Yquem.

'Let's leave it all to her. She'll probably snuggle down with Hugh under the duvet on the futon. We're fine here with Kitty's outlying relations.'

'Can I afford them?'

'I daresay not but let's take stock in the New Year when the snowdrops are out.'

They muddled through the evening with many humble complaints from Lizzie: 'It's not for me. I'm worried about your grand guests.'

'So am I. So am I. So am I,' sang Muriel to herself as she and Peter interlocked in their comfortable bed.

Chapter 9

It was perishing when Muriel woke. Dark, too, and she lit a candle. She tiptoed from the room leaving Peter and Monopoly to sleep and lighted her way with a torch to the bathroom where barely a trickle of water came from either tap at the basin.

The royal party was due to arrive in the afternoon and with no telephone she was overpowered by anxiety for the needs of these privileged people. Believing herself to hear Lizzie's teeth chatter when passing her bedroom door, Muriel shuddered but there was no sound of vomiting.

She lit her way down the stairs and, in the hall, spotted an envelope on the floor near to the front door. It shone white against the darkness around her and the grim blackness of the Christmas tree.

Inside the envelope was a written message, written, she presumed, by some local service; police or post-office. It read:

'Clarence House has been trying to contact you by telephone. A spokesman for Queen Elizabeth, the Queen

Mother, has been wishing to confirm to you that she and her entourage will be arriving at Bradstow Manor at approximately four p.m. today. They are all enjoying the prospect of their visit and Her Majesty wants it to be known that her only special request is that the house be warm and the party be seated by three p.m. on Christmas Day to watch her daughter, the Queen, give her annual broadcast to the nation.'

Muriel shook. No power for the Queen's broadcast. She dreaded the sound of the click-click-click of Lizzie's high-heeled shoes as she groped her way down the stairs, dripping candle grease and moaning about the cold.

No one was about as she reread the ominous instructions from Clarence House by the light of her torch.

This space of time, allowing her to be alone in the house, was heaven sent. She managed, with trials, to get a fire going in Peter's study and flung his cigarette butts onto the flames. As she acted, she thought how tremendous and wondrous it was to have his backing.

The house awoke.

Kitty brimmed with information.

She had collided with Phyllis in the yard and had learnt that Cleopatra's cot had been moved from the barn to the squash court where she, Phyllis, was to look after both Hugh and the baby. 'Although, I daresay, she intends to nip over here when royalty arrives. Good riddance if you ask me. You should see what she's made away with from here for their comforts.'

Phyllis out of the way; Hugh and Cleopatra looked after; Marco and Flavia free to cavort with Tommy Tiddler at The Bell. Things were working out. Muriel thanked Kitty.

As both women rejoiced at the turn of events there was a moment of triumphant astonishment. The lights came on. Power restored. They had returned from the brink of disaster.

Lizzie tripped into the room, pale with cold, at that very moment.

'Will I be able to have a bath now? I'm frozen stiff.'

She encapsulated a peculiar mixture – halfway between humble and assertive.

'Yes, Lizzie, but probably not yet. Let's go to the kitchen and stand near the cooker. I gather that's warming up.'

Lizzie able to watch 'soaps'! The Queen Mother's small refrigerator cooling gin and vodka. The Queen on television.

The telephone rang in celebration. It was Delilah.

'We're so happy for you, Muriel. Dawson was blue with cold writing his sermon for tomorrow. Talking of which, I've had a call from the organist – as soon as the wire was mended as a matter of fact – and she wondered whether, er, it might be appropriate to play the National Anthem before the service begins?'

Peter and Monopoly were in the study and enjoying themselves when Muriel told Peter of Delilah's query.

'Tell them to play "Thy Majesty How Bright". We'll have to get Mummy there on time.'

The telephone rang again. It was someone from the local police station wishing to check on details for the royal visit. The officer was in a jovial mood and added, after fixing an appointment, 'The Queen would have to pay a handsome ransom if either of these ladies got themselves kidnapped. I daresay she'd do as much for the bow-wows.'

Muriel hadn't catered for kidnap.

Lizzie asked, 'Sorry to be a bore but do I have to curtsey every time they come into the room or just morning and evening?'

Peter replied, 'Every time. Every time they sit down or get up.'

All was in uproar for the next few hours. No sign, though, from the dependants in the outhouses although Phyllis was reported to be gallivanting to and fro with baskets full of delicacies and appearing well pleased with life.

Delilah rang several times more and detectives, some of them girls wearing ponytails, came and went to check quarters.

Lizzie wasn't able to settle and packed and repacked

chocolates for the visitors, lamenting that she had nothing for 'Cunty' or 'Farty'. Muriel hadn't warned her.

'What a foul thing to call them.' Peter reminded her that it was because King George VI had not been capable of pronouncing his 'r' s that 'Cunty's' soubriquet had come about. She was actually called Miss Crunchard. By the same token Miss Farthing was known as 'Farty'. The late King, it was said, had also often confused friends by referring to his 'wank'.

The guests arrived at the front door on the dot of four and the household waited to greet them on the steps. Muriel wondered how many relations Kitty had collected together.

Dulcie stood, gruff and bowing from the waist as a frail and bent Queen Elizabeth climbed out of the Daimler with much help from Moggan and Cunty who, in Muriel's view, had aged since her last visit. Phyllis was there too – curtseying and dressed to kill.

Soon they were all in the hall. Queen Elizabeth well wrapped in furs and dark feathers, smiling wanly as the household fell to its knees. Princess Matilda, towering above them all, smiled too through thin, cracked, red lips. Her straight yellowish hair sprouted from under a fur beret – like Ken Dodd's – as she walked with a wanton gloom of deep-set melancholy that stretched through her shoes to wherever she stepped.

Dulcie muttered – intentionally inaudible, but suffering from deeply buried anxiety, 'Lot of bloody nonsense. Snobs. That's what they are. High and mighty and it is my belief that the elderly lady passed wind as I bowed to her. As for those two with disgusting names. Absolutely disgusting.'

They all stood like this for a short time as Cunty asked about the luggage. One case was full of presents 'mostly for each other' she said with reverence, and must be delivered to Princess Matilda's bedroom. Dulcie charged off with it muttering, 'They're a bloody mean lot. It's a well-known fact.'

Lizzie stood to attention too and wondered if they had brought anything for her; whether they would appreciate her expensive chocolates.

Peace and quiet spooked the house as the ladies and their helpers inspected their rooms.

Lizzie sat very close to the television in Peter's study gazing at an Australian comedy serial as Peter smoked and smiled.

Muriel checked on the drawing room where they were to assemble for 'cocktails', as Mambles always called an evening drink, at seven o'clock. She made sure that a silver-framed photograph of Queen Elizabeth, taken to mark her ninetieth birthday, was suitably displayed upon a lacquer chest. She had been presented with it on a former visit and had been made to understand that it had constituted a special privilege. Mambles had lowered her eyes, 'Mummy doesn't normally give a photograph unless she stays the night.'

On that occasion, however, she had, between lunch and dinner, spent several hours on a spare-room bed having not long since undergone a small operation to remove a piece of chicken bone from her oesophagus.

The frame of the photograph shone and Muriel was pleased.

When Matilda spoke of her mother she always mouthed the one word 'Mummy' although she never failed to refer to her sisters as 'the Queen and Princess Margaret'.

At exactly seven o'clock they came into the drawing room. 'Mummy' walking slowly with a stick and wearing diamonds. Mambles, also wearing diamonds, looked – in contrast to her mother – gigantic and walked lackadaisically; feet turned inwards.

In her free hand Her Majesty carried a flat parcel wrapped in tissue paper. She handed it to Muriel who tried to curtsey and thank at the same time. From the feel of the thing she suspected it of being another of the signed photographs dished out at the time of the ninetieth birthday and, before opening it and holding it in one hand, made for the lacquer chest where, deftly, she

shoved the one she already possessed behind a poin-
settia in a china *cachepot*. One of them would make a
good placatory present for Delilah if the visitors failed to
attend church service.

Mambles spoke clearly, 'By the way, Muriel, I forgot
to tell you that Mummy's on a special diet. She can't eat
chocolate.'

Lizzie gave out a squeal as her knees cracked under a
curtsey. 'I'd bought you some, Ma'am. For Christmas.
They were very expensive.'

Mummy smiled a radiant smile 'They'll do for Cunty
and Farty.'

Both Cunty and Farty appeared; each leading a small
dog. Sir Walter Raleigh, property of the Queen Mother,
and Jubilee, property of Princess Matilda. Each lady
handed each dog, both on leads, to their owner.

Mummy asked of no one in particular: 'Did you know
that the real Sir Walter Raleigh was hanged? Something
about a treaty with Spain. I've always taken an interest in
the doings of the late King's forebears.'

Monopoly eyed both dogs with scorn, turned to show
an unfriendly bottom and stayed close to Peter who was
excused from bowing since he could see neither of the
royal ladies.

A table for five was laid for dinner in the dining room.
It was to be enlarged the next day for lunch when they

were to be joined by Hugh, Marco, Flavia and Cleopatra.

Peter, the only man, sat between Mambles and her mother. Lizzie, decked in clasps and shawls, was seated between Muriel and Mambles.

Mambles asked Lizzie if she still ran a junk shop. Lizzie replied 'antiques' and that she had sold it at a profit and was terribly worried about the chocolates. 'Muriel ought to have warned me.'

Mambles said, 'She didn't know,' and lost whatever interest she had held.

Both royal ladies refused the first-rate wine, bequeathed, with everything else that he owned, to Muriel by the late Jerome Atkins. They preferred whisky – even at meals. The old lady asked about watching the Queen's speech. Had it been arranged? Muriel panicked for fear that Christmas lunch might not be finished in time. Marco and Flavia were certain to be late and hold things up. Then there were always complications about feeding Cleopatra. Mambles detested children although she had insisted on becoming the baby's godmother. She was certain to ask about a Christening and nothing had been mentioned by Marco about one although Delilah frequently brought the subject up.

Mummy turned to Peter and confided that she shared with her daughter, the Queen, a passion for the turf. 'Although,' she continued to smile, 'donkeys were my first love. When I became engaged to the Duke of York, there was a photograph, that hit every headline, of me as a small child riding on a donkey at my home in Angus.'

'There are two in the paddock here. Neddy and Ryan.'

'If it's fine I should like to be introduced to them tomorrow.'

Considering the enormity of events, the evening was low-key. Guests were tired after the journey and Muriel was tired after preparing for them. Peter never altered and Lizzie stayed brightly excited; geared into an emotional condition by the failure of having bought unacceptable and expensive chocolates. Nobody went to bed late but there was a disembodied energy in the air; each one of those present in personal anticipation as to what they might give or receive the following day.

Chapter 10

Soon after midday, Mummy, Mambles, Cunty, Farty and Peter (not one of whom had managed to grace the morning service) gathered round the tree under which were stacked shiny packets. Mummy had been provided with a straight-backed chair, throne-like, and sat upon it beaming in regal triumph. On her knee she held two small parcels – looking as if they'd been wrapped in a shop.

'One for Cunty and one for Farty.' She enunciated very clearly – particularly for a person of over ninety.

Muriel and Lizzie, fresh from church where a disappointed congregation had scanned front pews, joined the group as Cunty and Farty upon hearing their names called out darted forward, both in a curious way, seeming to walk backwards as had been the custom in days gone by whenever in the presence of any HRH. In fact it was forward that they walked before curtseying.

Mummy handed them identical packets and said soothing words to each. Something relating to loyalty. As they opened their presents in calm respect, they didn't move any of their four feet and kept their four eyes on the form of their seated employer. Each woman found from within the wrapping identical bottle-openers with ivory handles. Being abstemious, neither woman had use for such objects and Mummy and Mambles only drank spirits. Nonetheless they were deeply grateful and each assured Her Majesty that her own particular bottle-opener was to be treasured as they signalled to each other to preserve the wrapping.

Mambles, tall and cross, said, 'My turn next,' and handed a packet to Muriel. It was floppy and told of fabric. When Muriel opened it she found, to marginal disappointment, that it contained a Japanese dressing gown. Mambles had been allowed to raid the Queen's hidden store of presents from foreigners. 'Those awful Nips keep giving them to the Queen and I was allowed to take my pick for once.' The pick she had been allowed must have been from a crate and some years back. Muriel already had four of them – given to her on birthdays and other special occasions. At least, now, she had room for storage.

Lizzie, too, was given a Japanese dressing gown and was genuinely delighted. Planning, as she unwrapped it, to let it be known that she wore a kimono that, albeit briefly and untouched by her, had belonged to the Queen.

Hugh arrived dressed, as he had been in church, very much for the occasion in an old tweed suit and waistcoat – rather tight. He had (or maybe it was Phyllis) been hard at work polishing his shoes and wore an over-bright tie to add a trendy touch. He bowed at the waist before the royal ladies and handed each a small parcel. They put them immediately to one side – accustomed as they were to gifts being opened at a later time by interested servants.

Mummy was gratified by the gravity of Hugh's deferential bow and told him of a programme she had heard on the wireless – just after prayers – that morning. 'It was on the topic of something called premature ejaculation. Has that anything to do with early rising? It seemed the wife objected. I was always pleased when King George VI rose earlier than I did. He had so many functions to perform. It was aggravating when Cunty came in and switched the programme off.'

Flavia joined them – wearing very high-heeled shoes and a great deal of beige lace that clung tightly to her figure. She was followed by Marco, tie askew and suit crumpled, full of verve; bounding with bows and bonhomie.

No sign of Cleopatra.

Mummy asked, 'Where's the baby? With nanny, I expect, for luncheon.'

Marco explained, 'Phyllis is feeding her lunch with the others in the kitchen. Great service, by the way, Ma.' He kissed his mother who then ran quickly to the kitchen to ensure that the high-chair had been removed from the dining room.

Mambles joined in: 'I told Mummy about Cleopatra. She asked me if we need see her more than once. Diana and Fergie took their children to tea at Clarence House the other day and Mummy found them tiring.'

Cunty and Farty, piled high with chocolates – many boxes having been pressed on the allergic old lady – left for the kitchen. The others opened several more kimonos and bottle-openers before they took their seats in the dining room.

Peter, negotiating for harmony, leant across to his brother Hugh.

'Hugh, as it's fine, would you take Queen Elizabeth to visit the donkeys this afternoon? After the Queen's speech of course.'

'Certainly, Ma'am.' He looked to her with courage and a red face and told her that he gleaned great pleasure from living so close to Neddy and Ryan in the paddock although they were sometimes noisy.

Mambles said, 'Count me out. I'll wait by the fire and then go upstairs with Mummy when they get back. She'll need a rest before we prepare for dinner.'

Muriel, agitated, asked if they would come down well before dinnertime. She had invited Dawson and Delilah for a drink and had no wish to let them down.

Mambles teased, 'Have you got something up your sleeve, Muriel? People, I suppose, dying to meet us. We always cause a stir. I do hope it's not that ghastly vicar and his wife who's son let down our poor Greek cousins.' Muriel had to admit that Mambles had guessed at the truth.

'I think I shall risk it and go as a biscuit,' Mambles said, stretching her eyes and smiling as she always did when revelling in the delivery of random snatches.

Her mother beamed and told Hugh: 'We may not always be popular but we are very important to the country.'

Hugh, bedazzled, leant towards her and answered, 'I hear what you say.' She stared at him. 'I should hope so. I have always spoken clearly.'

Lizzie, still in an anxious state, made a set at Hugh. There was little to be lost. 'I'm dying to visit the squash court. I actually used to play squash at school. I was frightfully good.'

Hugh, not wishing to cross his wires, Phyllis having installed herself on his balcony, muttered something about 'tomorrow' whereupon Lizzie became jumpy and said she could tell she wasn't wanted.

Monopoly stayed in Muriel and Peter's bedroom. He loathed Sir Walter Raleigh and Jubilee and did not enjoy the presence of Hugh in the house. There had been a time when he had worshipped him; had pined when he had so cruelly disappeared – but now his loyalty had swung to Muriel and to Peter. Hugh made him jittery.

Muriel raced them through turkey and Christmas pudding, well laced with brandy butter, and cheeses. Desperate with the timing of events.

They walked to the drawing room where a fire was lit and where a television had been placed, centrally, especially for the purpose of the day.

The Queen Mother didn't sit. 'Easier to stand and wait to sit down after the National Anthem.'

Mambles flopped onto the sofa. She loathed it when Mummy showed respect to her sister and writhed under the burden of her fading position in the family. Nonetheless, when the Anthem began, she did rise to her feet and stood, solemn but angry, until it faded and a picture of the Queen, radiant in a flowered frock and hair arranged like two cornets – one on each side of her temple – appeared on the screen. She sat at a desk and spoke in clear, child-like tones, telling of a Christmas party held in the mews at Buckingham Palace. 'Even the horses in their stables are serenaded by the carol singers and seem to be aware that something quite special is happening – as they were on that happy July day when my son and daughter-in-law were married and they drew the carriages through cheerful crowds thronging the London streets.'

Mambles looked daggers. Mummy reverent and Hugh terrifically impressed.

Lizzie said, 'I'm sorry but I worship the Queen. Perhaps it's because she's been anointed.'

As she spoke she knew she had put her foot in it with the sour-faced Mambles and her hands shook.

As they began to revive after the excitement, the door flew open and Kitty summoned Muriel with a nod of patient irritation.

Muriel went, at once, to join her and to learn that Sonia wanted an urgent word in the abandoned office. Why was the no-longer-employed Sonia not at home enjoying her own Christmas in her own way?

In the cold office, Sonia quivered and held a struggling Sir Walter Raleigh in her arms. Sir Walter had, somehow, given his mistress the slip. 'He's damaged,' she shrieked, 'I'm calling the vet.'

Muriel told her to desist until the dog's owner had been consulted. Sonia mumbled something incoherent about the dog having chased a cat. Muriel carried Sir Walter, now quiet and still, in her arms and headed back to the drawing room where Queen Elizabeth was gracious and pronounced him 'fit as a flea'.

Uncharacteristically and infuriatingly for Muriel, Sir Walter somehow managed to wander off again – his being so small nobody noticed. After less than five minutes Sonia was in the room, crying maniacally and squeezing Sir Walter very nearly to death in her stubby arms.

'Sir Walter,' Muriel said as everyone stared, 'is okay Sonia. No need to worry.'

'This dog could be responsible for the death of a cat. There are three elderly cats here and nobody cares.' She shook and shivered and raced out, dropping the dog, in the throes of a helpless outburst.

Princess Matilda asked, 'Does she know who we are?'

Queen Elizabeth rose above these earthly matters and basked in her own serenity.

Excusing herself, Muriel, carrying a cup of coffee, made a run for the office (after admitting to all that she was mortified and horrified by the accusations made against Sir Walter) where Sonia sat in floods tirading against the heartlessness of royalty.

'Corin is prone to heart attacks if chased. Those bland faces in your drawing room. Nobody listens. Nobody cares. They bring these dogs down here with no thought for me. What with that and your mongrel.'

Muriel threw the remains of her coffee into Sonia's face. She knew it to be a mistake but she'd put up with rudeness, bolshiness, unwillingness and poisoned atmosphere for too long and loathed cats.

As Sonia, shrivelled and doused in coffee, cowered behind a chair, Muriel said, 'The cats will have to go. Joint ownership doesn't work. I know that Corin belongs half to you and half to Dulcie but I must have freedom. It's my home. I'd been looking forward to the afternoon and showing my visitors the donkeys.'

'I'm sure you had.'

'I'll find a good home for Corin if you won't take her yourself. That, of course, would be the best solution.'

'I couldn't. Not living on my busy road.'

'Sorry, Sonia, but you seem to think she's (Corin was a female cat) equally unsafe here. Lots of dogs visit; strays, village dogs, friends' dogs. We can't watch her round the clock as you can and Dulcie doesn't worry.'

Then, down on her knees, went Sonia – tears streaming. 'Spare Corin. Please spare Corin. I can't be responsible for her losing her home. Spare her. Spare her.'

Muriel, wishing she hadn't thrown the coffee, told Sonia to go home.

'I'm never coming back. They'll believe you. Nobody will believe me.' It sounded as if she planned to report the coffee incident.

The number of people planning to show Mummy the donkeys had increased. Marco (but not Flavia whose face was flushed) decided to join in. Cunty and Farty were sent for, also Moggan – who had been keeping the kitchen in fits with imitations of Prince Charles.

Hugh was the established leader and gave Mummy his arm as they walked, extremely slowly, across gravel and wet grass to the gate of the paddock where not only the donkeys but also Dulcie lived.

Dulcie stood on the top step of her van. A cat (called Plod but known as Irene) clung around her neck and bowed with her as the party stopped at a good viewing point. No sign of Corin suffering a near heart attack.

A terrible noise was the first thing to catch the attention of the onlookers; a noise like the labour pains of giants. A rasping, groaning, throaty bellow that came from a large grey mass that moved. Neddy was humping his son, Ryan. Heaving – up, down, up, over, down and even under. Dulcie, her rasping near to drowning incestuous noises, addressed herself to the house party.

'You've chosen a bloody awful day to show Her Grace a bit of country life. That'll teach you to hobnob with Hanoverians.'

Cunty and Farty ran to protect their mistresses' eyes. Her sight was poor and she didn't understand why they crowded in on her. 'Cunty. Farty. Go away. I've come to see the donkeys. I used to ride on one when I was a child in Angus.'

The heaving and humping became louder and louder – as did Dulcie's expletives. Hugh rounded the group together and said something soothing in explanation.

Mummy muttered words that sounded like 'the beasts of the field' as Dulcie, well pleased, shouted, 'Entertainment over for the day, I trust.'

Muriel stayed behind in the paddock. She needed to have a word with Dulcie about Corin and Sonia's explosion. Dreaded it but felt it must be tackled. Dulcie stuck her stomach out, 'She's not having Corin and that's flat. I can keep her safe from a bunch of miserable little town-mouse dogs if anyone can.'

'You will have to sort it out with Sonia but she is no longer to be involved with the welfare of cats on my land.' Muriel became masterful for a moment. She took a step backwards and crunched the empty shell of a snail with her wellington boot. It had been taught to her in a biology class that snails were hermaphrodites, hibernated and were, if such a thing was feasible in a snail, right-handed. Dulcie showed no will to hibernate and shook her right fist.

Muriel, standing still for many minutes, said 'Hibernate. Hermaphrodite' to herself over and over again until it gave her a headache.

Dulcie looked over Plod's back and her shoulder towards the stream and beyond. 'I daresay you are wondering about them trees.'

Behind the paddock was a copse where trees, bare in December, stood, spindly and spare. In their branches clustered great, dark bundles of densely packed twigs. A bit like herons' nests but rounder and more solid. They differed in size from that of a small football to a giant balloon.

Dulcie followed Muriel's eyes: 'Those bundles of twigs are no more than malignant growths. If you'd got it into your head they were mistletoe you were completely wrong. Stuff and nonsense. Mistletoe and fairy lights. What is more the whole neighbourhood will be down with malignant growths if you don't do bloody something about it.'

The foul form of Eric stole up beside them. 'Don't you listen. Cut those out and you'll be upsetting the balance of nature.'

Malignant growths or the balance of nature.

Muriel returned to the house and the many quandaries that awaited her.

Chapter 11

Lizzie was down first in the early evening. Soon after came Muriel and Peter who prepared for Dawson and Delilah and their visit. Lizzie was short – not much above five feet. Her hairdresser-helped dark hair turned under, pageboy style, at the bottom of her neck. Her eyes were large and blue and, at times, almost vacant. Nose straight but wide of nostril. Mouth huge and inviting entertainment. She dressed well – draping scarves and bracelets. Lizzie's appearance showed careful nonchalance but, when she spoke, the image changed to eagerness.

'Are the royals going to be down in time for the rector?'

'Who knows?'

'Is Hugh, poor Hugh, invited for dinner this evening? I did suggest paying him a call but he was frightfully putting off.'

Lizzie could be astoundingly touchy. 'Why? Why, do you think? We always got on tremendously well in the old days.'

Muriel, speaking quietly to temper crossness, said, 'Of course he likes you. It's just that he's up to no good with Phyllis – my housekeeper.'

'That fright in nylon? Poor Hugh.' She sided with men. Muriel squirmed to be reminded of Hugh's undignified position – although he'd certainly asked for it.

Monopoly, driven to distraction by the presence of the visiting dogs who gave themselves airs, kept mostly to the bedroom.

There came a loud 'Cooee.'

Dawson and Delilah were dressed for a party and arrived many minutes earlier than expected. Dawson, in dog collar, asked for a gin and tonic while Delilah opted for champagne and Muriel hoped she wouldn't get too silly before the visitors from upstairs condescended to appear.

Delilah told Lizzie that Dawson had a lovely story up his sleeve for them. Something to do with a cartoon in which the Queen Mother wore a gown and mortar board. There had been a caption saying 'To crown it all'. Lizzie was jumpy with the prospect of solecisms. Peter hoped for them. Muriel was beyond caring. Nonetheless she was pleased by Dawson having an anecdote up his sleeve and Delilah, all curls and teeth, smiled having practised curtseys.

She could not count on the ladies coming down before supper was announced; particularly after Mummy's experiences with the donkeys – not to mention Sonia and Sir Walter Raleigh.

But the miracle did happen. There was a hush as the door opened and Phyllis, having belted to and fro from the squash court, ushered the guests of honour into the drawing room. Delilah and Lizzie curtseyed. Peter, at a nudge from Lizzie, nodded his head and Muriel, unnerved, remained upright. Mambles darted her a critical look and Mummy beamed on all present.

Delilah tackled an obdurate Mambles. 'We are all thrilled to have Muriel at the manor. Of course we are very broadminded people here in Bradstow but, well, what with her husband in the squash court and her, well …'

'That's the way the world goes round.' Mambles loved 'sayings' always believing herself to have invented them.

'Then. She's made one or two little mistakes. You have influence. If only she could come to us for pastoral advice. Letting that metal detector into the grounds …'

In the very early days Muriel had allowed a Salvation Army member to search for coins in a nearby field. It turned out that he was an unpopular figure in the neighbourhood and given to thieving. He'd had to be banned access.

Getting no reply this time, Delilah swivelled and asked Muriel, 'Might it be *comme il bien* to present Her Majesty with some of Dawson's home-brewed beer? I left a bottle of it in the hall so as to ask your advice first. We so love the thought of it being served at Clarence House.'

Not for the first time Muriel thought, Christ, what a pickle.

Marco bounced in – eager for happenings. 'Flav's at Dad's place and Phyllis is having kittens; bathing Cleopatra as well as tarting up dinner for Dad. Peach blossom room fragrance and all.'

'That's gorgeous for your daddy,' Delilah cried as Dawson ran through the mortar board anecdote – directing it at Peter. 'Well. It was some time back. Her Majesty was collecting some doctorate or other. I take an interest in these things – being an academic.'

Delilah overheard and brightened at his words. 'Yes. Dawson's an academic. I'm just the rector's wife.'

Lizzie, unnerved not to be the centre of attention, went close to Muriel and demanded, 'Are the newspapers delivered tomorrow?'

'Tomorrow? Boxing Day. I rather doubt it.'

'I must have the — (she mentioned the name of a right-wing daily paper). It has the best telly guide. Can you find out?'

Delilah swung round. 'No papers on Boxing Day. Not delivered to the door at any rate. It could be that they are printed. The supermarket would be your best bet.'

'Where is it? Will anyone be going past? Is it too far to walk?'

'Four to five miles at a guess.'

'Will someone be going in the morning?'

She inched closer to Muriel who was trying to synchronise her party and let thoughts of luncheon the following day attack her.

Hugh, Tommy Tiddler and the goosing judge invaded her brain. The royal ladies, it turned out, were scheduled to leave after lunch. They had to be at Windsor Castle in time for dinner but Lizzie had made no mention of her departure. Mambles lost her punchiness when Mummy was around and went into regression, occasionally sucking her thumb.

Mummy was more important; more in the public eye than herself. She had been ousted by the Queen's children, their wives and descendants.

Delilah ran, backing as she left the room, to the hall, returning with the bottle of home-brewed beer that she presented to the seated Mummy.

When the party was over – when Dawson and Delilah had left, when Marco had hopped back to the squash court to help eat Phyllis's quiche Lorraine and down wine from Muriel's cellar – the ladies and Peter dined, not particularly merrily, in candlelight in the dining room.

Alone in her room with Peter, Muriel shrugged off the happenings of the day and opened an anthology of love poems that Peter had given her as a Christmas present.

It excited her that Peter, in spite of blindness, organised matters such as presents.

The introduction thrilled and fascinated her. The author wrote of the altering complexities of love. 'I love you. You love me. I used to love you. You don't love me. I want to sleep with you. Here we are in bed together. I hate you. You've betrayed me. I want to kill you. Oh! No! I *have killed* you.'

She was in bed with Peter and loved him. He loved her. They wanted to be in bed together. Hugh had betrayed her. She wasn't sure if she had betrayed him. She didn't exactly want to kill him and sincerely hoped that she wouldn't but she loathed having him in the squash court and was sickened each time he approached or attempted tenderness with her. Loathed it.

Chapter 12

Mambles sent word that she wished to see Muriel in her bedroom before breakfast was brought to her on a tray at nine-thirty.

She was propped on her pillows and her mouth had already been swiped across with bright lipstick. Her hair was in a net and Jubilee snuffled under one of her thick white arms.

'I needed someone to talk to.'

The floor was scattered with splinters of white – alongside larger bits of broken china.

'I was given horrid presents yesterday. Really horrid. I smashed the one your awful ex-husband gave me. Was he playing some sort of trick?'

Muriel picked up a few of the larger fragments and pieced them together. It had, until smashed by Mambles, been a large and hideous mug with the words 'Old Fart' printed on the side. It was hard to imagine how Mambles had broken it so thoroughly – made, as it was, from hard but tinny porcelain. With a shock of dismay she realised what had happened. Hugh, concentrating on his stately bow, had handed Mambles a packet that had just been handed to him by Marco assuming that they were both in a part of a royal chain of presentation.

She looked at a large bit that had formed the base of the mug and read the logo. '1st for fun.'

'Oh Mambles. It was for Hugh. Marco was giving it to his father. They must have got muddled.'

'Cunty opened it for me last night after I came up to bed. Neither of us knew what to say. I threw it against the skirting when she'd gone.'

She insisted that Muriel sit on her bed. 'None of that curtseying now there's no one to witness.' Jubilee went on wriggling.

Mambles's efforts to beguile faded and her eyes went very black. 'If you only knew how much I hate Cunty.'

'Cunty?'

'Yes. The way she sucks up and has to have goat's milk – or is that Farty? She treats Jubilee as if he was her own dog.'

'I don't understand why you mind about goat's milk but I'm sure she doesn't suck up exactly. Just reveres. As for Jubilee. She does quite a lot of the looking after.'

'Now you're taking her side.' Mambles started to cry and asked for a vodka. Then she told Muriel to summon Cunty. 'Jubilee needs to be taken walkies.'

'Why don't you get dressed and we could go for a walk

together with Monopoly? It's cold but it might cheer you up.'

'If you ever talk about cheering me up again I'll scream and frighten Mummy. You know how I hate being cheered up. Why is everything so horrid? Everybody's cross and sad. Why can't I have a drink when I want one?'

Muriel heard the shrill cheep of Lizzie's voice and the tic-tac-tic of her high-heeled shoes on the landing.

'I'll send Cunty up but, Mambles, don't be beastly to her.'

'I'll be as beastly as I like,' she said as she rolled her eyes and reached for a cigarette and a vast box that contained jewels beside a smaller box jammed with pills of different colours.

Muriel plodded down the back stairs in order to avoid Lizzie who used the handsome front ones and wondered if she understood any of the inner workings of any of her visitors. She went in search of Peter. If she sat on the floor at his feet there was a chance that he might place his hand heavily on the top of her head and stop it spinning. He did and she almost recovered.

Chapter 13

As the senior ladies breakfasted in their rooms, Lizzie raced to the squash court where she found Hugh and Phyllis dallying over coffee cups as Cleopatra, tidily adorned, played with plastic in the pen. Marco stood beside it, encouraging her movements. He straightened up when Lizzie entered and demanded, straight out, 'Is anyone here going to the supermarket? I know it never closes.'

Hugh did have the use of an old car, battered and provided for him by Muriel. Marco, too, had shabby transport and Phyllis was allowed use of either one. Lizzie's hopes were high.

'Surely one of you must be going to a shop.'

The three adults looked blank. What with lunch at the manor house and Hugh's small larder now well stocked, there was no need on Boxing Day to venture out.

Hugh, pleasantly reminded of Lizzie's artful appearance and sparkling manner, asked, 'Is it urgent? Perhaps I could run you there.'

Phyllis said, 'I've got duties this morning so you'll

be needed here for Cleopatra. That is to say, unless her parents are prepared to do the job.'

Marco shifted. 'Sorry. Flav's not at her best this morning and I've got to tidy the barn. Get our show on the road. You know. Get our act together.'

Lizzie was unrelenting and she, Hugh and Cleopatra (strapped into the baby seat behind) set off to buy a copy of the Boxing Day tabloid.

As they left Phyllis pursed her lips and said to Lizzie, 'Very well, and you can see to baby's bedtime tonight.'

After buying the newspaper Hugh returned Lizzie to the big house where she flattered him to excess. 'I can't thank you enough. Muriel is so obstinate. It's almost as if she doesn't want her guests to have what they need. I really don't understand it. If I had a huge grand house with masses of servants I'd want them to feel at home.'

Hugh, in his slighted position, agreed but with restraint since the arrangement suited him for the time being.

Triumphantly armed with the newspaper that bulged with supplements Lizzie went into the house, thanking Hugh again and saying that she looked forward to seeing him at lunchtime.

Muriel was aggravated when she saw a copy of the loathsome paper flaunted on the hall table but her hands were full and she didn't speak; merely rebelled within to see that Lizzie had had her way; had satisfied her want and that Hugh had assisted her.

Newspapers were, in fact, delivered to the door but none to Lizzie's liking so Lizzie felt justified and gloated over having inched nearer to Hugh; not that she wanted to have to put Cleopatra to bed. The project needed thought.

As she considered, Cunty came down the staircase; sharp-eyed, red-nosed and in a dither. 'Mrs Cottle. Her Majesty believes there to be a rat or some other type of rodent in her bedroom. She detected a loud, squeaky sound coming from under the floorboard. Miss Farthing and I have pulled all the furniture from the skirting and opened up a trunk containing old clothing. Fancy dress, I imagine. An antique trunk.'

'What am I supposed to do?'

'Well. Her Majesty suggested you go and sit with her for a while. You might know if it is or is not some form of vermin in there. Possibly under the carpet.'

Was she a landlady as well as a hostess? Providing beds, baths, curtains, light, heat and hanging space was clearly not enough. Her duties, it transpired, lay well beyond her open-housed munificence. If only they were all paying guests instead of costing her a slice of her indefinite fortune.

Queen Elizabeth, hair in a net and wearing an eye

shade, sat propped up on pillows, Cunty close beside her on an upright chair.

Muriel was asked to sit on a divan at the foot of the bed and to listen for sounds. They heard nothing whatsoever as they sat still as stones for over half an hour.

'It must have died. That or be unconscious,' the old lady suggested. Muriel apologised for the distress and begged to be set free to find out what had happened below and how the Boxing Day lunch was progressing. Before taking up her post in the hall she went to find Kitty in the kitchen.

'That Dulcie. She ought to have oiled the pulley. Squeaks like an animal it does – when she tugs on it. It's her own oilskin garments she's drying. Why she has to do it at this time – and on Boxing Day – I'll never know. I wouldn't be surprised if the old lady – Her Majesty I mean – hadn't been disturbed by it. Her hearing is fairly sound.'

All in a rush the lunch party was upon them. Those staying in the house were assembled. Hugh and Tommy Tiddler arrived more or less simultaneously – soon followed by the judge. Both Hugh and the judge dressed tidily; each suit a trifle too tight. But Tommy Tiddler!

No one, least of all Muriel, had anticipated such an apparition. Scent and stole. He did not wear the brooch made up of copulating goats but a diamante fairy seated on an enamel toadstool. He whispered to Hugh, 'One was creamy round the crutch when one dressed for this. Nearly parked a crafty. I hope one hasn't overdone it but one was rather pretty when one was young.'

Hugh, appalled to be coupled with this freak, walked towards Lizzie who wanted to thank him again for having taken her to the supermarket.

The judge, having made his obeisances, also leered at her. His face was lopsided as if he'd suffered a mild stroke. She sparkled and said, 'Isn't this fantastic. Muriel at home to nobs.' Then, animatedly to both pairs of ears, 'I'm allergic to royalty myself. Actually allergic. I feel physically sick when they're in the room. I can't wait for this afternoon when they leave.'

The two men, terrified but impressed, laughed loudly but glanced at the causes of the allergy as they did so – wondering which side their bread was likely to be buttered.

Tommy puzzled Mummy who didn't know if she spoke to a man or a woman. It was all a bit much at her age – what with Dulcie in the van. He said, 'One does love Christmas and putting on all one's bits. What it must be to wear a crown. The mind boggles.'

Queen Elizabeth, rising above such matters, said, 'I think there was a rat in my room.'

Mambles was being charmed by Marco but Flavia had failed to appear. 'Still getting into her gear,' he explained, 'that and the little one who's to be fed in the kitchen again. Good on Ma. And Pa come to that. We'll soon be off the hook if this Phyllis thing works out.'

'Phyllis thing?' Mambles asked.

'Yes. Pa and Phyllis. A bit of a twosome. Suits us as she does all the dirty work in the squash court.'

'Hope it's not too much of a squash,' Mambles opened her eyes very wide and was happy to have made a joke although she did not approve of cross currents with lower orders.

Marco laughed lustily and Muriel began to hope that all was going well.

Tommy's fingers neared Mummy's diamond brooch. It had large baroque pearls hanging from it and she put up a hand for protection. He feigned a swoon. 'What a celestial piece. Would that you'd do swappums with my fairy,' but she didn't appear to understand his words.

A table plan had been worked out by Peter. Mummy sat at the head. Hugh on her right – then Mambles, Tommy Tiddler, Muriel and the judge at the end – opposite Mummy. To the judge's right sat Flavia, then Peter, Lizzie, Marco and back to Mummy.

Marco talked to Mummy of her importance to the country as Lizzie struggled with Peter, cross not to be beside Hugh or, at least, the crooked-faced judge.

Mambles asked Hugh, 'Has Marco turned over a new

leaf since becoming a father?' Hugh, taken aback with Marco only a few feet away, replied, 'Yes. The country suits him. Lessens the peer pressure.' Mambles who, in spite of Mummy's efforts had never received pressure from peers, sat nonplussed.

Flavia, also downcast by her place at table, pouted and drank.

Muriel was saddened that Mummy and Mambles were in no way struck by the splendour of the dining room or of what Mambles had, on other occasions, spoken of as 'nice things'.

Tommy Tiddler asked Mambles what it was like to be a bird in a gilded cage. He began to sing, lifting his eyes to the ceiling and a glass to his lips.

Muriel loathed it all. Mercifully the entourage, it turned out, was set to depart in the afternoon. Return to some sort of reason. She yearned to settle, quietly with Peter and Monopoly, to wallow in the thrill of her unexpected fortune; to sum up her duties, possibly to buy a horse.

She heard snippets of conversation as courses came and went.

There was a sixpenny bit in Mummy's slice of pudding left over from the day before and fried. She asked Hugh to polish it up for her. It was wrapped tightly in a piece of greaseproof paper and, as she swallowed brandy butter, she asked, 'Is it the late King, my husband, or my daughter, the Queen, on the coin?'

Hugh reproachful and at a loose end. Lizzie staying indefinitely. Marco, Flavia and Cleopatra. Phyllis's shifting position added to anxieties whilst, in the short term, solved some.

Dulcie menacing; donkeys incestuous; Sonia insane; Dawson and Delilah a constant tug at her conscience. What, she asked herself, is there to hope for? Hugh and Lizzie? It didn't do to picture Lizzie permanently in the squash court but, hang on, she did have a flat in London and now that Monopoly loathed Hugh, there was no interest for him in the country. But what of Phyllis? Too many conundrums.

Mummy and Mambles took up a whole page in the visitors' book. Cunty, Farty and Moggan didn't sign their names. It was, according to Mambles, inappropriate, although they had stayed in the house.

When the hoo-ha of their departure was over, the judge turned his wonky face to Lizzie and asked, 'And how long, dear lady, are you staying here?'

Lizzie, hunted, said that Muriel had not mentioned a date for her departure. 'I feel like a displaced person. Not knowing if I'm wanted.'

'Come come, dear lady, I was hoping you might make up a bridge four this evening. Do you have wheels?'

'Wheels? No but I'm sure someone …'

Muriel, quickly, said, 'We'll try to get you there. There and back. Let me have a quick think.'

An evening alone with Peter promised her happiness and hope.

The judge made a suggestion. 'Why don't you come back with me now and spend the night? I'll return you to camp in the morning.'

Lizzie, notwithstanding doubt, jumped at it. Hugh otherwise occupied. Muriel soppy with Peter.

'I'll make a quick dart and pack. Muriel, you don't mind, do you? You know I worship bridge.'

Muriel returned to the anthology of love poems and the fireside with Peter and Monopoly.

Poems aside, there was an uncomfortable amount for them to discuss. Muriel's fierce and utter disenchantment with Hugh was a tricky one. Peter had no wish to further rubbish his brother. He inclined to the belief that, whatever his true feelings about Hugh, he had rubbished him enough in that he lived in blissful contentment with Muriel.

She hankered to be shot of her husband, his very presence a blight, and was irritated to remember that Mambles had bamboozled her into housing him in the absence of other solutions. She wondered whether the young man who had been so disturbed on seeing the picture hanging above the piano in the hall, had come to any conclusions on its provenance. Might the ownership of that still tempt Hugh into considering a divorce?

Marco and Flavia, drunk and dissatisfied, dumping the demanding baby on her at inconvenient hours.

Anxiety-ridden Lizzie, temporarily appeased by her bridge-playing sleepover with the goosing, widowed, ex-judge, was to return the next morning for an indefinite number of days.

Phyllis, destabilising in her triple role: housekeeper, husband's mistress and nurserymaid to her granddaughter.

She wondered whether she might not be happy as an 'Avon Lady' trudging up to the doors of others instead of owning so many doors herself.

Her mind focused on Lizzie. Lizzie had, in spite of being no longer young, scampered up the stairs to pack her overnight needs; including the Queen's kimono, in readiness for her journey with the judge.

She had waved goodbye with neurotic brightness from the window of his old Mercedes as her escort strained to fasten the safety belt round his person – larger since lunch.

Chapter 14

Lizzie took stock. Hugh was no certainty. Muriel and Peter were excluding in their closeness to each other. The judge was worth a try and, on that path, she knew that she was certain to conquer. She was lively as they drove and she entertained Judge Jones (Jack) with tales of Muriel's past and to an edited degree her own. She told him that she had been married, years before, to an eligible man but that she had left him for a Dutch magnate of vast wealth. The Dutch magnate had, in truth, let her down (she didn't mention this in the Mercedes) but not before handing over several pieces of valuable jewellery (which he tried, and failed, to regain – also not mentioned in the Mercedes) and setting her up in an antique shop in the Kings Road; the shop in which Muriel had worked for her before the shocking oddity of inheriting Bradstow Manor.

'He was frightfully attractive.' She spoke to the judge of the Dutchman, 'But absolutely hopeless in bed.'

The judge changed gear and colour.

'My word. I bet you're a good judge. Judge – ha-ha. Lovely lady like you.'

They drew up on gravel beside a well-built house. It was bleak but not shabby. A lot of laurels.

Inside, Lizzie looked about her and realised that it wouldn't quite do. Not in the long run. A wide passage held several large mahogany cabinets displaying sets of china glistening with gold leaf and over-restored paintings of dim-looking ancestors. Large purple and blue rugs; a live Labrador in a bleak, flowerless sitting room; unlit fire. There were several framed photographs on stands. One, clearly, of the judge's own wedding in a London church with several grown-up bridesmaids. He wore a carnation in his buttonhole and the bride looked timid. There was another of, presumably, his wife at her coming out party; tight hair and flouncy frock. One photograph Lizzie noticed in particular was of three grinning teenage youths. It certainly wouldn't do.

On a low table stood a tarnished silver box. Lizzie opened it and found it to be half full of cigarettes – in likelihood dating from the days of Judge Jack's wife. He said that he never smoked, other than accepting the odd cigar when offered.

Lizzie picked one out. It was dry and had gone an odd shade of brown. She lit it with a fiddly match from a tiny box that was also encased in tarnished silver. She hadn't smoked a cigarette for years but took one as a ploy to find distance between herself and the judge. Her huge eyes watered and her throat went dry and scratchy as she took small puffs and tried to remember which fingers to use.

'So,' he said, 'welcome to the humble home. It's a bit lonely without Sandra and the boys can't get home much these days. I had hoped to see them over Christmas but it didn't work out. But needs must and I have an excellent helper. She'll be cooking the dinner tonight. Leaves it for me to serve. Not quite the fancy fare over at Bradstow Manor – but let me show you your quarters.'

The quarters were large but damp. Watercolours of flower beds by the score hung heavily from picture hooks and Lizzie asked herself what the hell she was doing there – little realising that his impulse-invitation had also thrown Judge Jones into a quandary. His wife's cousin, Betsy, and her foolish gossiping husband were to have brought a Christmas visitor with them to make up a bridge four but, only that morning, she had slipped a disc and was lying wailing on her bed. Betsy had rung Judge Jones early that day to warn him about bridge but, egged on by Dennis, said that they planned to leave her to wail and to venture out themselves, bridge or no bridge. They knew that Jack had lunched at Bradstow Manor that day in the company of royal ladies and they were anxious for scraps he might let fall before the event faded. When, in a salacious second, he had asked Lizzie to make up the bridge four, he had been thinking firstly that she, although not young, was damned attractive but secondly of the game.

As he left her at the door of the spare room, he knew that it wouldn't do to talk too openly about the lunch party in front of Muriel's friend. It was sure to be reported to Muriel and he would stand accused of making capital out of his privilege. Lizzie had said, truthfully or not, that she was 'allergic' to royalty and was sure to discourage his account.

Dennis was likely to be drunk and to pump him and to accuse him of sticking to protocol if he refused to tell all.

He missed Sandra and her quiet ways; her support of him when he had made an idiot of himself – even her subsequent decline and determined amorous rejection of him when he failed to find himself a place on the New Year's Honour's list.

As he brooded in his bedroom and removed his tiepin, Lizzie popped on the Queen's kimono and walked across the passage to a bathroom. Were she to end up here, she decided, she would insist on *en suite*.

Dennis and Betsy arrived on time. He was red in the face. Wore a dark red cardigan and brightly coloured tweed trousers. Betsy was rather pretty; dressed in a gypsy way and wearing boots. One thing was clear. They were both astounded to see Lizzie there. An unknown woman, terrifically dressy, standing in Sandra's sitting room. Never even heard her mentioned.

'Tell all!' Dennis lit a cigarette. 'We want to hear about you mingling with the mighty.'

Lizzie, wearing jewelled clasps, once the property of the Dutch tycoon, rose in frenzy.

'I was there too. Muriel is my best friend. It was frightfully boring. I'm totally allergic to royalty. I can't think why Muriel asked me.' Which, of course, she hadn't done. 'But I worship bridge so, when ...' – for a second she didn't remember the judge's name – 'when Jack invited me to stay the night I was totally delighted. I'm mad about bridge; not that I'm very good,' she added on a note of caution.

Dennis said, 'Quick work, Jack. Did you only meet this lovely lady this very day?'

Betsy, keen on peacekeeping, said hurriedly, 'What a good idea. I've always loved last-minute plans – not that we ever make any. We feared it was farewell to bridge when poor Rosemary slipped her disc in the night. Can't think how but she's doubled up.' Lizzie suspected Dennis of having paid her a midnight visit and of dislocating some portion of her spine.

The judge, having had time to adjust, said, 'It was fun. Lovely place. Funny set-up, though.'

'Hanky panky?' asked Dennis.

'I daresay you could say so. Husband in an outhouse. His brother at the manor – that sort of thing.' He looked nervously at Lizzie.

'But – the royals?' urged Dennis. 'Did you have to bow? What do you call them? Spill the beans, old boy.'

The group had to move into the dining room where stew and mashed potatoes had been left on a hotplate. Lizzie noticed that a pat of butter on the table showed small smears of marmalade. The musty mildew of a widower hung over the whole house. Her half-formed project must be abandoned or transformed. Candles of uneven length had certainly been used before – but not often. Salt cellars not even half full.

Judge Jones, though, was a friendly host and talked as fast as he knew how of the church service he had attended on Christmas Day.

It was not good enough for Dennis who, tucking in to stew, returned to witnessed highlights.

'Does that newcomer at Bradstow have nobs there all the time? What's her name for a start?'

Lizzie told them the tale of Muriel's inheritance, of Hugh's defection and of Peter's moving in. Everything but what they angled for.

Chat was for a short time frozen as Betsy and Dennis both hoped for Lizzie's departure in the morning to be a final one. Not much point if she prevented Jack from spilling the beans – anyway they had already paired him off with Rosemary. If only she hadn't slipped a disc.

Dennis, though, wasn't to be silenced. 'Was that dreadful Tommy Trout there? He gives me the willies. Not that I'm anti-gay. In fact I rather like them. Betsy,' he turned to Lizzie, 'loves them. He held up a hand and counted on his fingers a) No threat b) Often artistic c) Useful as escorts – or walkers as I believe they are now called. A little bit of Tommy goes a long way though. Like lavatory paper. All right when it's new but not so good once it's been used.'

Betsy tried to laugh. Dennis, with a hiccup looked to Lizzie: 'My wife's an intellectual, you see. Belongs to a book club. That sort of thing.'

After supper they played bridge but not inspiringly and, not very late, the visitors left to stuff their guest with painkillers.

Alone with Judge Jones, Lizzie worried about the rest of the evening. She accepted a glass of brandy – hoping not to regret those last sips as she swallowed. Judge Jones told her that he was interested in local history. The Dutch and so forth. She touched her necklace that had come to her via the Dutch magnate.

His wife, he told her, had been a first class citizen. 'Craft shows and all that' – that the boys were all in jobs in London, 'that is to say that Malcolm is overseas at the moment.'

They each had a young lady. 'Live-in these days I'm afraid. Partly due to the economy.'

Lizzie was stupefyingly bored and wondered if Phyllis lay with Hugh on the duvet in the squash court.

Hugh, if nothing else, was attractive and hadn't had a stroke.

When Judge Jones had turned off the downstairs lights and stood with Lizzie on the landing he said, wistfully, 'I know these are early days but perhaps, who knows, we might see more of each other.'

She sidled and felt for the door handle – but he was upon her, lunging into lechery and starting to lick her face with a wet tongue that darted and slithered as he frisked and fondled her. Lizzie, although she knew full well that she had invited, even encouraged, such treatment – was displeased.

'You and me,' he whispered in slobbery gasps. 'You're very attractive.'

'I know but I'm sorry.' Lizzie seldom spoke without saying 'I'm sorry' but this time she meant it – and for herself.

'Sandra,' he whimpered, 'Sandra turned against me. No warning. One night when I tried to …'

Lizzie said 'I'm sorry' again as she tried to turn the

door handle. It was slippery and didn't engage properly.

'The next time I tried, she made more excuses.'

This time the handle turned and she half-opened the door to her bedroom but Judge Jones clung and went on trying to lick her. Lizzie said, 'I'm sorry but, look, I'm tired and I've got a lover already. Anyway. I've got a bad back.'

'Back! It's not the back I want. It's the …'

He'd gone too far, far too far; even for Lizzie who had tried most things. She made it to the other side of the door and closed it firmly.

After removing jewellery she went to bed. Her struggle to stay awake and think things through was defeated and, head on damp pillow, she fell asleep.

The same trace of marmalade appeared on the same butter dish at breakfast where the burnt-down candles stood on the same spot as they had done the night before. Coffee and toast waited on a hotplate but no human being appeared to help. It struck Lizzie that, perhaps, no such person existed – that the judge had prepared it all himself in advance – including stew and mashed potatoes. Protected his image by saying there was a 'good lady' in the wings. Even made up the damp beds himself. She decided on cutting and running. She was flipped if she was going to toil in that bleak house surrounded by laurels and rabbits.

He asked her if she had slept well, adding that he had gone out like a light. She pictured him hot and snoring like a bull and was impatient to be off. It seemed that he had no awareness of the failures of the night before.

In the Mercedes, he asked her if they might meet in London. 'Go for a bite somewhere perhaps.' He didn't mention a lick.

She thanked him, said goodbye after giving him her telephone number with one faulty digit and raced into the hall where Muriel stood among the piano legs and beaded stools, planning to take Monopoly for a walk.

'How did it go?'

'Well. He did pounce if that's what you wondered.'

'It wasn't but did you like it?'

'I certainly did not. He was desperate to have an affair.'

Judge Jones constituted no startling conquest but Lizzie enjoyed any trophy – however meagre. She had full and justified confidence when it came to attracting men. It was holding their interest that usually defeated her.

'It was sweet of you, Muriel, but please don't introduce me to any more nutters like that. Damp sheets and marmalade on the butter.'

Lizzie, in high heels, tottered out after Muriel and Monopoly. It was cold and snow hung in the sky. Lizzie was frozen in spite of a thick coat but, against other instincts, wanted to keep talking. Muriel was her only hope for the present, Peter being feeble at chat.

They skirted the squash court, the barn, Dulcie and the disgraceful donkeys and walked towards the stream over hard short grass.

'Seriously, Muriel,' Lizzie asked through chattering teeth, 'what exactly is going on between Hugh and that housekeeper of yours?'

'Don't know. Can only guess. She was completely taken in by Roger a year or so ago. Packed and left – but I've told you all about that.'

'Yes. Yes. I know all that. But what's going on now? Now. With Hugh?'

'Frankly, Lizzie, I'd like to strangle Hugh with my bare hands. It's bad enough having him so near, let alone his making up to Phyllis.'

Lizzie, as Muriel knew, sided with men.

'Poor Hugh. He must feel so humiliated. No status.'

Lizzie set store by status – never having, it seemed to her, achieved it.

Muriel presumed that, whatever it was, she did, now, have some herself and loathed each second of it. But her heart bumped as she spied a cluster of early snowdrops and her spirit rebelled against the discussion of 'pouncing' and such-like – now that she was a grandmother.

What was to be done with them all? If only, at least, Marco and Flavia had a hoover.

'Would it be all right if I stayed until after the New Year? You haven't got any more grand people coming, have you?'

'No. Nobody.' There was nothing for it living, as she did, in this merciless house. Lizzie intending to capture Hugh.

Chapter 15

Marco and Flavia, in the hooverless barn, drank white wine and talked over possibilities. Flavia was undomesticated and the large space was desolate. Marco had an instinct for style but no leaning towards detail. The playpen now lived in the squash court as did the ancient perambulator. The cot was still in Cleopatra's own room in the barn. Phyllis tended to return her at bedtime so she could cook up something tasty for Hugh.

'If only Ma could pension Uncle Peter off.' Marco's expression was cross and his eyebrows met above bleary eyes. 'Tell you what, Flav. Let's get Roger down and set the cat among the pigeons. He'd have a crack at Lizzie and put Pa on his metal. Hoof out that fright Phyllis.'

Roger had caused havoc amongst them all in the past.

'What about Cleopatra then?' She pouted and her voice transformed into a wail. 'I won't survive without Phyllis.'

'I'll dream something up. We'll have a New Year's Eve party and ask them all. Tommy Tiddler, Pa, Phyllis, Lizzie, Uncle Peter, the judge. The whole shooting match.

Rector and Delilah – the son who drops his trousers on public transport. Wine from Ma's cellar. World first.'

Flavia brightened. She loved a party – even if this wasn't exactly her idea of one but she had a flair for instant effect. She knew just where to find flags and damask cloths at the top of her mother-in-law's house. A house to belong, presumably, one day to Marco. It was imperative to stick it out.

'Give Roger a ring.'

Meanwhile Hugh was restless. He'd like to have run Lizzie to a local cinema or a pub lunch. She was game and sparky and 'on' for adventure. But there was Phyllis who had moved in and clung. She had extracted unfulfillable promises and had taken advantage by luring him into criticism of Muriel. 'I can't cope with the way she treats you.' He was compromised and she'd taken over Cleopatra. He found that hindering – a toddler squawking in the squash court. Nonetheless he enjoyed tormenting Muriel with a soppy look of reminder that they shared a grandchild.

Phyllis fussed on the balcony – sorting the futon. Cleopatra lay in her pen playing with a cuddly toy given to her by Cunty for Christmas.

Hugh went to the window and spied Muriel, Monopoly and Lizzie walking near the stream. He pulled a scarf round his neck and buttoned up his coat.

Muriel, dragooned by her mother into courtesy since birth, had had lapses but now reverted and greeted Hugh civilly. He was encouraged and said that he needed to speak with her and that Lizzie was more than entitled to listen in.

'The situation, Muriel. It can't go on.'

'Which one?'

'Phyllis. Cleopatra. They've moved in on me. Your granddaughter too, Muriel.'

Lizzie, although juddering with cold, was on the job. 'It must be seriously awful for you. She's too dreadful for words – that Phyllis. Awful name too. Why don't you come and stay with me in London for a few days? Clear the air. After the New Year, that is.'

None of them knew of the party that Marco and Flavia brewed up. Hugh pondered. He couldn't remember when the New Year was. Lizzie's invitation, though, was thrilling. He half closed his eyes and, turning towards her, said, '*Enchantée Madame.*' Muriel willed him to open his eyes and speak in English but said nothing.

There was no holding Lizzie although she was shivering in the cold air. 'Do come. Stay as long as you like. I've only got a tiny spare room – not quite Muriel's problem I know.' Her laugh tinkled, 'But there's always masses to do in London.'

'Far too long since I hit the metropolis.' He opened

his eyes this time but still spoke partly in French. 'Lovely *Londres*. I do miss it.'

Hugh left them. He was not keen to be snubbed by Monopoly and so delighted by Lizzie's invitation that he was not going to risk a retraction. He hoped that Muriel might give him something to spend in London. They were still married to each other but she'd never said anything about sharing assets since she came into her astounding inheritance. That picture. True. She had promised it to him and there was a chance … She also gave him the rent from her London house but time spent with Lizzie was sure to run him into the red.

Muriel was nonplussed. 'Are you sure, Lizzie? It's very kind and all that.'

'Seriously, Muriel. I suggested it entirely for your sake. I do feel sorry for Hugh, of course, but I know you're dying to be alone with Peter. A break will make it easier for Hugh to hoof out that creature.'

'He did ask for it. Poor Phyllis. She's anyone's and Hugh took full advantage.'

'He was lonely. Anyway – I'll give him a frightfully good time. Ask people to dinner or something.'

Lizzie had never asked Muriel to dinner in all the years she'd known her.

Back indoors, when Peter and Muriel were alone, he said, 'Perfect. It won't last or even be a success but it will

give us a breather and we can give Phyllis a holiday – if
she has anywhere to go.'

Chapter 16

Roger, the media man, was too canny to accept Marco and Flavia's invitation to spend the New Year with them.

He'd blown it badly with Muriel on his last visit – even introducing a pretender to her kingdom.

Muriel, during one of her periodic bouts of loneliness when married to Hugh and before coming to an understanding with Peter, had fallen for Roger in an unruly way but not before introducing him to her son and daughter-in-law. He drank heavily – which fact, as well as picking his nose deeply and disgustingly, had cured Muriel of last remnants of infatuation and, moreover, had created a lasting allergy. He had then turned to Flavia for a frenzied fling that had fizzled out when Muriel inherited Bradstow Manor and Flavia decided to take part in anticipating the pickings.

Flavia was disappointed when Roger refused their invitation. She was keen for distraction, flirtation and hashish. Nonetheless she continued to plan the party.

Marco made steady steps to Muriel's cellar, calling to Flavia when he returned with baskets full of bottles, 'I say, old girl. What about this? Pre-war. 1929 Cheval Blanc,' as he stacked the shed that stood at the back of the barn.

Flavia raided the attic for flags and fabrics. Dulcie was to be heard offering violent advice as more and more ancient objects were lugged down the stairs, through the hall and across the courtyard; sometimes in the dark. 'Get the bloody corpse upright,' she bellowed as she humped a tailor's dummy, with Flavia's help, over a rolled-up carpet. It was not to be rolled up for long. The carpet, too, was taken to the barn where Marco draped it over trestle tables to create a bar.

Muriel, aware of Dulcie's heaving, acted on Peter's advice and ignored all noises.

Hugh, Phyllis and Cleopatra continued as before in the squash court – but Hugh with more enthusiasm since knowing that he had a London season ahead of him and that soon he was to dislodge Phyllis. He had not decided when or how to break the news to her but he did, at least, know that a plot was hatched.

Marco told his already suspecting mother of the planned party as she meandered about in the hall and plucked dead heads off flowers. She was pleased that her earlier anxieties about her status as intruder no longer bothered her. She had firmed up.

'Flav's found some fantastic things in the attic. Nothing you'd need. Maids uniforms – aprons and all. Thought we might slap Phyllis and Dulcie into them for the evening. And we've found wondrous treasures in the cellar. Should we ask the dreary old rector and his troupe?'

Again and for the countless time, she longed to be left in peace; alone to discover treasures in the attic. Marco and Flavia were running before they could walk and, again, with the use of her legs.

The evening for Muriel and Peter, in spite of Lizzie's grating voice and scratchy mood, sped along. Lizzie, much lit up by the failure of her evening with Judge Jones and the tales she was able to tell, was also enlivened by the planning of the forthcoming visit from Hugh in London; not that she ever knew what to do with people when they did arrive on her doorstep. In fact she seldom invited anyone to anything – preferring to stay away from her own quarters.

'So,' she asked with chirpy verve, 'when are you planning to turn me out?'

Peter, coolly enraged by the implications of her question and guessing at the hysterical way she strung out her neck as she asked it – veins everywhere, he imagined, replied, 'New Year's Day.'

'No. Seriously, I'm sorry but it's hopeless trying to travel on a Bank Holiday. Can I stay till Tuesday?'

'Of course,' Muriel downhearted, spoke firmly. 'But Hugh will be hot on your heels, don't forget.'

'You're not cross with me are you, Muriel? Peter. She's no right to be cross with me, has she? He's your brother after all. Doesn't he deserve some treats?'

Peter laughed. 'I think he's had plenty of them in his time but I daresay he could do with a few more and who, Lizzie, but you are better able to provide them?'

Muriel put Monopoly out before going to bed.

Chapter 17

It was New Year's Eve and the barn was very cold in spite of Marco's efforts with blow-heaters bought for the occasion from an electrical store. Draughts snaked in and over the floor. There was no porch or inner door to protect the vast room from wind that rushed in as guests arrived. Flavia, wearing a floating, transparent, impractical idiocy, had arranged for Cleopatra to spend the night at the Manor House with Peter keeping an ear. He didn't go, as a rule, to parties and was pleased with an excuse to stay away from this one.

Phyllis, thus, was free to join in although Marco had been against her being invited.

'She'll dress to the nines in nylon and make a fool of Pa. Cramp his style with Lizzie and put Ma in a strop.'

Muriel and Lizzie were the first to arrive. Muriel was dazed to see so many objects from her attic on display; trunks draped in tapestries, banners; the amputated leg of an elephant. Chamber pots, bedpans, stuffed owls; a taxidermised hare. She noticed, too, some rather remarkable pieces of furniture – a large silver chest clanking, no doubt, with knives, forks and spoons. Georgian probably. A screen covered in faded lilies of the valley; several formal portraits – tacked onto the walls. Her son and his wife had had a field day.

With much help from Dulcie, Marco and Flavia, after days of looting, had, to be sure, made the stark barn look exotic and eerie. The tailor's dummy had been dressed up as Dame Edna Everage; huge red spectacles and a mauve wig.

Lizzie, sparkling in spangles, laughed edgily as she looked around – avid to sight Hugh. She was excited by the prospect of tantalising Judge Jones too. Fearful, nonetheless, that she might fail to dazzle, she clung to Muriel whilst thirsting to be free of her. In face of locals it suited her to be seen to be Muriel's best friend.

Before long the barn was heaving and Hugh's arrival was barely noticed either by Muriel or Lizzie who had been backed into a corner by Tommy Tiddler. He had come decked and perfumed; hoping to find royal people. He smacked his lips and said to Lizzie, 'What about these trinkets and *bibelots*. One doesn't often venture into the abodes of the blessed. I'm afraid the *humble home* will seem very shoddy when any of you lot pay a call – after all this finery.' He spoke coyly as he referred to his cottage.

Phyllis, unstoppably in tow, stood beside Hugh as Lizzie inched towards them leaving Tommy 'to goggle'.

Lizzie asked Hugh, low-toned, 'Have you told Phyllis that you're coming to stay with me in London?'

He cleared his throat as was his habit and answered, 'Yes. Yes. Of course. No problem.'

Phyllis, with 'problem' etched onto her face, jumped: 'Did I hear mention of my name?' Hugh tried to bring her forward; further into the circle as Delilah barged up to promote a woman who had arrived with her at the party. 'I must introduce you to your new neighbour Melanie. She's only just moved in – gorgeous little cottage beyond the paddocks. She's going to need to socialise.'

Hugh was polite and marginally attracted by Melanie's mysteriously witch-like manner. He asked her where she lived in London and what brought her to Lincolnshire.

'I don't know really. It's odd, isn't it? I bought the cottage on a whim. Pressure of social life in London. I don't know anyone here. My friends,' she looked modest, 'are mostly writers or in showbiz.'

Phyllis edged towards Lizzie. 'I did hear mention of my name. Can you kindly put me in the picture?'

'The picture? I just wondered if you were up to date about Hugh coming to stay with me in London for a bit. He's lonely here as you know.'

'Lonely? He's a shit. Just like the rest of them. It was a bad day when she inherited this place.'

The lips of a moth-nibbled kudu glowered at them all

from a wall where it hung, insecurely, from a hook.

'Poets too. Artistic people,' Melanie told Hugh. 'Are there any intellectuals here tonight?' Hugh was not at all sure how to reply. The place was palpitating among the antlers. Dulcie and Flavia between them had worked wonders on stepladders with a Black-and-Decker.

Marco brimmed glasses and told no one in particular that 'Auld Lang Syne' was upon them. Time they formed a circle. No one listened or heard.

'*Alimentari,* my dear Watson,' he said to his father as he handed him a mushroom on a stick. Muriel didn't remember ever having felt so muddled.

Delilah's voice overtopped the rest. 'Gorgeous. Thank you. We mustn't stay late.' Alastair stood beside the effigy of Dame Edna; transfixed as his mother went on, 'One or two parishioners always pass away at this time of year and Dawson's lovely with the dying.'

Defying Delilah's vocal effects, a weird noise obliterated all else.

Phyllis, thanks to Marco, having drunk as many glasses of 1929 Cheval Blanc as time had allowed, screamed at concert pitch.

For an instant Muriel, who turned in panic, thought that Phyllis was standing on her head. It was near to the ground; jerking on that of a tiger, and her legs kicked up and down; up and down like drummer's sticks.

'Who'd have been looking after the child, poor little bitch, if I hadn't come to the rescue?' Amorphous groans escaped from her mouth, her knee joints, her shoulders, her toes.

Hugh approached. 'Ahem. Er, Phyllis. You've been great. Terrific.'

'And now what? I'll give you terrific. I knew that Mrs Lizzie had her eye on you. Not for the first time either.'

The room was silent but for Phyllis and all listened.

'Not according to the bits and bobs I've picked up from Mr Hugh on the pillow.' She reverted to formality as she kicked and sobbed into the tiger's teeth.

Flavia was excited and pirouetted in her finery.

Delilah called for Dawson and pastoral care. 'Come quickly, Dawson. She's one of God's creatures and she's in need.'

Dulcie, keen for assault, brushed Delilah aside and grabbed Phyllis, picked her up and threw her over one shoulder. 'Bloody little man-eating tart. That's all she's ever been after. Looking after the baby my eye. Just worming her way in with Grandpa.'

She stumped out into the icy night with Phyllis a furious captive on her back.

Flavia stopped pirouetting and started to cry. 'What will we do? What about Cleopatra? Who's going to look after her? Muriel's a useless grandmother.'

Tommy Tiddler wrapped his poncho round her shoulder. 'There. Dry those naughty little tears. One's out of a job and would make a lovely nanny. Grey felt hat and all. Bound to be one in that attic. Treasure trove.'

'Would you? Really?'

'Nanny Tiddler at your service. One might have to take her to the *humble* for some of the sessions. One cooks at home for freezers. Quiche Lorraine's and starters.'

Flavia viewed the future more hopefully. Anyone would do.

'What about that poof poison he sprays himself with? Don't want Cleopatra reeking of that.' Marco shifted on his feet but rejoiced that help was at hand.

The party, such as it had been, began to subside.

Lizzie was twitchy and said, four times, 'But Hugh. You said you'd told her,' before trailing behind Muriel who hurried to relate all to Peter. She had barely taken in that Judge Jones had not put in an appearance. They left Hugh making a date to meet Melanie for lunch in London during his stay with Lizzie.

Tommy, very tipsy, chain-smoking and triumphant, asked if he might be permitted to touch up the pram. 'Trellis-work or posies *appliquéd* to the hood. One can work wonders with spray paint.'

For once Peter went to bed before Muriel. She sat in his study and pondered – wishing that many things were other than they were. She struggled to order her brain to dismiss glum thoughts and unsolvable problems. Her brain refused to obey her and, before lying down in bed beside Peter, she swallowed a strong sleeping pill. A box full of them had been procured for her by Mambles who gained perks and special benefits from a retired royal physician.

Chapter 18

After breakfast Peter sat in his armchair, shifting it to pull away from the heat of the fire from which his eyes saw no spark or flame, and tried to deny himself the indulgence of gloating over his brother's plight and, instead, probed the poison of their past as childhood brothers.

With Hugh now humiliated, living without luxuries in the squash court whilst he, Peter, relaxed in a position of contentment with Hugh's wife almost always beside him, it was as well to remember that Hugh had had earlier control.

They were the only two children of a father who hated snow and Christmas, talked like a tycoon but failed to make a fortune and a fluttering, freckled mother who blinked and fussed and had inherited a tumbledown estate near London from a great-aunt. The house was large, Georgian, faced due north and needed repair. Peter remembered it with agonising precision and was glad, as his brain clicked to the present, that Bradstow Manor had been in reasonable repair when Muriel had been faced with the same type of unexpected windfall. His mind threaded back again. The ha-ha, the field that flourished in nettles, the Wellingtonia burdened with broken branches, the soggy grass tennis court and a haunted yew walk. It was wartime and bombing a remorseless threat. No lights were to be shown; black blinds were barely lifted during the day and sticky paper zigzagged over windowpanes to stop glass splintering during a raid. A pail stood on every landing to catch drips when pipes thawed after freezing. Gas masks lay under sofas where they were unlikely to be found in emergency and they ate boiled squirrel and stinging nettle soup. Outside there were dilapidated stables and a sketchy number of people to help in home or garden. Men and boys at war.

The boys' mother worked hard to keep things going but had poor organisational skills. Since the house was large Peter, as he thought back, found it bemusing that he and Hugh had been made to share a bedroom. That had been easily the worst thing about the war – sharing a room with Hugh whose brutal ghoulishness knew no limit.

Neither parent had influence – for a start Peter barely understood what either of them tried to say but Hugh was blood-curdlingly comprehensible.

Although their features were alike, the boys differed greatly in childish development. Hugh was taller than was average for his age. Peter grew slowly and was chubby – in spite of rationing.

Sometimes, at night, doodlebugs went silent and the household evacuated to the cellar for fear of calamity. They were always ill-prepared and dreadfully cold. Doodlebug nights, as Peter cast his mind back, were the best, for then, at least, he was not alone with Hugh. In the image he held he was no more than six or seven years old.

Anything had been happier than the chilly hours at Hugh's mercy. Sheets were clammy and paint on the walls, an air-force blue, peeled – leaving jutting-out flakes that formed faces of witches with snot pouring from their noses in the near darkness.

No sooner were they both in bed than Hugh started his favourite game. It was called 'how do you know?' and drove Peter almost insane with despondency.

When he hid his head in the lumpy pillow, he used to try being nice and often said, 'Good night, Hugh. I'm going to sleep.'

'How do you know?'

'Cos I always do.'

'How do you know you always do?'

'Cos I want to.'

'How do you know you want to?'

This torment went on and on and on – often starting again when Hugh woke.

Peter, at that time, had a morbid fear of dead animals

of which there always seemed to be several around the place; a stiffened frog by the pond, a jellified dead baby bird with eyes bulging onto the path; a mouse floating in a water butt. One summer morning there was a rat, newly dead, beside the grass court that had no lines as they had run out of paint. Peter circled wide so as to avoid it but Hugh picked it up and swung it by the tail – squash – into Peter's face. He retched and cried. Hugh called out, 'Crybaby. Crybaby. Wet. Wet. Wet.' Then he thought again. 'But you are wet. You wet your bed. I'm telling everyone.' Peter had once done this when he had whooping cough and knew that Hugh exaggerated since there was no one much to tell but he dreaded his father hearing of it when he came home in a rough mood. It didn't make any difference that it had happened ages before – the wet bed.

On the night of the rat Hugh suggested that they race each other to bed, adding, 'If you get in first I won't play "how do you know".'

Inspired with hope Peter hurled himself into bed, pushed his legs to the bottom where they met with soft, wet, and horrible slush. The rat was there and bleeding.

There was another thing. Peter yearned to learn how to knit. Their nanny, a pink-faced kleptomaniac, knitted jumpers for her long-term fiancé, George, who worked as a porter at the railway station. On her half day off she was employed at the morgue where she enjoyed laying corpses out. 'First I squeeze out the body juices,' she would tell him, 'then I cross their arms over their chests and sing "Abide with me".'

Peter wanted to ask her to teach him to knit but always lost his nerve for fear that Hugh might find out. The urge became very strong and he tried with twigs but found them too knobbly. And he had no wool. He managed to get hold, though, of two long pencils and a card of darning yarn but never really achieved results. He struggled with it on a bench under one of the Wellingtonias but one morning he was discovered there by Hugh who shouted in glee, 'Nit Wit. Nit Wit. Nit Wit. But I'll call you Knit Wet as you wet your bed.'

In a poor Lancashire accent he danced and began to sing a George Formby song starting: 'I'm a little nitwit – knitting all day,' and ending: 'You should see me knit. One plain. One purl. A pleasant occupation for a good little girl.'

Life improved when Hugh was sent to boarding school. During his time away Peter talked his mother into moving him into a small room of his own and nearer to hers.

Chapter 19

The parents had at least seen the sense to send them to different boarding schools and in the holidays the boys avoided each other. Peter tried to please Hugh when he could but Hugh, even as he grew older, was set on a course of deliberate misunderstanding.

Once as they parted on a school train platform Peter said, 'Have a good term, Hugh.'

'Why shouldn't I have a good term? Are you insinuating that I'm likely to have a bad one?'

Nothing worked.

Later, when the disintegrating house was sold and the parents had moved into a lifeless one in Hampstead, Peter tried to avoid coinciding with Hugh when they visited.

Hugh did well in his working life and became a Member of Parliament whilst Peter, although knowing that his confidence had not been totally destroyed, knew too that he would never achieve worldly success. He worked for a publisher and wrote verse in his spare time.

When the brothers were twenty-seven and twenty-five respectively, their mother rang Peter. 'Isn't it exciting? Hugh has just told me that he is engaged to be married. He's bringing his fiancée, name of Muriel (your father doesn't care for it), for tea on Thursday and we both feel that you should be here to welcome her into the family.'

Hugh came in to the cheerless sitting room with the most spellbinding girl Peter had ever seen. Perfect in his eyes. Dark and plump and merry in a slightly terror-ridden manner. Hugh had pulled it off. Never would Peter meet anyone comparable.

He fell in love and said, 'Hugh. Congratulations. I hope you'll be very happy.'

'Why shouldn't I be, if I may ask? Are you suggesting that I won't be?'

Muriel was talking shyly to their father at the time and didn't hear the brothers' interchange. Peter wondered whether he was going to trip and fall – so besotted had he instantly become.

After that he kept away from the couple although, after the marriage, Muriel tried to include him in family gatherings which seldom took place. Occasionally they spoke on the telephone and one day Peter told her that he was not happy in his flat. Neighbours were noisy and it was dark. Within days she spotted a For Sale sign on a house a few doors from hers and suggested he buy it. Too near to Hugh but never could he be near enough to Muriel. He bought it without much delay or consideration.

Hugh and Muriel's marriage was going through a disastrous patch and Muriel took to calling in, pretty frequently, on Peter. He had never been so happy and, since neither he nor Muriel saw much of Hugh, there was no reason for feelings of guilt. They did not flirt with each other; just talked and smoked and smiled.

At a certain point, Peter became aware of slight headaches and flickering pressure from behind his eyes but made no move to see a doctor. In truth he was afraid to go out very often for fear that Muriel might call. He did not wish to risk missing a precious moment.

His sight went very suddenly. He saw only black and, at first, it seemed impossible that he was never to see again. Impossible even to light a cigarette. All impossible. His eyes were still in their sockets. That was something but perhaps they looked misty and white. What was Muriel to think when she saw him?

She did see him – every day and he did, at least, already know how beguiling she looked. He soon began to realise that the compassion released in Muriel made up for his huge and terrifying loss. He was happy and so, it certainly seemed, was she. She took him to any number of opticians but not one of them offered any convincing explanation. One said it might have been an apoplectic effusion in his brain. Another simply said it had been a stroke – an unusual one that had affected only his sight. Not his arms or legs.

And so, he said to himself as he heard the door open in his study – the rest is history.

Hugh sat down in a chair near to Peter's and, clearing his throat, began to speak.

'So, Peter. You are the lucky one now. You don't know what it is to be excluded – to have to live in an outhouse with you, you, swanning it in my wife's bed.'

'I'm sorry, Hugh.' It was easier now that he couldn't see the black rage that would spread into Hugh's eyes as he tormented him during childhood.

'It's the way things have worked out but I don't swan it. I keep very quiet.'

'So I should hope. I am pretty sure that half this house belongs to me. We're not divorced.'

Just then Monopoly walked across the carpet and settled by Peter's feet. Peter could feel fur brush his trouser leg and stretched out an arm to stroke the dog.

It was far too much for Hugh who exploded in the way he used to do.

'And my dog. You are vile. Vile. You've always been sneaky and vile.'

But Dulcie charged in. She had heard Hugh's raised voice and wanted some fun.

'You two. Fighting like babies. Ought to be ashamed of yourselves. Bloody awful the lot of you.'

Nothing was changed by the ordeal.

Chapter 20

It was impossible to get rid of Phyllis. She had been seriously deranged by Hugh's affection followed by defection and lay twisted on her bed – visited regularly by Dulcie who threw saucepans' full of water over her face and asked, 'What the hell did you expect? We all knew he was a prime figure in a scandal of a sexual nature. My mother was a district nurse and brought me up with an iron hand. Absolutely firm. I'm thankful to say, she advised me to have nothing whatsoever to do with men. Nothing whatsoever.'

The only mercy offered by Marco and Flavia's New Year's Eve party was that Judge Jones had not been present. He did not trust himself to the outer world and dreaded seeing Lizzie again. She had asked for it by thrusting herself at him but it had to be faced. He had made a fool of himself.

He wrote to Muriel the following day. 'Hail to my neighbour. Would that I could have seen the New Year in with you and your young. I had a blocked nose but I'm on the mend.

'I wonder if this is an appropriate moment to mention

this to you but a dicky-bird has told me that your comely housekeeper might be seeking another post and I find that, since the death of my dear Sandra, I would welcome …'

Peter said, 'Perfect. Let's take her over at once. She'd love to be goosed and he can lick her as much as he likes.'

Lizzie had not resisted spreading the tale of the licking outside the bedroom door.

Phyllis and her very few boxes were driven to the laurel-enclosed house by Joyce. Dulcie settled into the back of the car for the ride, snorting and assuring the two other women that she was 'not interested in whose posterior the judge does or does not fancy.'

Soon after this Hugh left for London. His visit was not a success. Lizzie was nervously sensitive owing to lack of much encouragement from Hugh although he had taken her to buy the newspaper on Boxing Day. She had done her best to animate him and had hoped to be barricaded with blandishments but Hugh was not inclined to kindle too fierce a flame in her, in spite of her sparkle, for he was looking forward to his lunch with Melanie who mixed with intellectuals and showbiz people. Phyllis had frightened him too.

He arrived at Lizzie's flat mid-morning. When he had seen his very small bedroom in the basement he hoped to be offered a cup of coffee.

'Lunch?' she asked. 'Shall we go out to lunch? There's a smart new Italian restaurant in Fulham.'

'I'll be roaming the streets at lunchtime. Tailors and so forth but, perhaps, we might meet up tonight?'

Lizzie said that she planned to be at home that evening.

Hugh met Melanie for lunch and found the situation awkward. She had assumed that they were to spend the rest of the day, and probably the night, together and became huffy when he explained that he owed the evening to Lizzie.

Lizzie was out and he let himself in with a latchkey that she had given him and decided to make himself a cup of tea. There was absolutely nothing whatsoever in the refrigerator. Nor in the cupboards – save for an elderly tin of chicken liver pâté. Not even a biscuit or a banana – let alone a packet of tea.

They were, as foretold, both in that first evening but Lizzie didn't offer him anything to eat.

'Seriously,' she said, 'I never eat anything from lunchtime onwards. Not until I go out for breakfast in the mornings – unless I'm meeting someone that is.'

Hugh offered to take her somewhere for dinner but she shied from it. She wanted to watch television. At seven o'clock, she told him, she always turned on the news – however horrible. On this occasion she and Hugh drank wine. Hugh had brought four bottles of the pre-war Cheval Blanc from Muriel's cellar, squirreled away by Phyllis, with him.

After the news, she fished out a video, an old 'soap' and together they watched that – drinking a fortune's worth of last drops.

Video over, Lizzie told Hugh that she was going to bed and he wondered if she expected him to make a move to snuggle up with her. He didn't want to. She irritated him and he was extremely hungry and a bit drunk. It was very unsatisfactory and he had no idea of what Lizzie's game was. She barely knew herself. In the aftermath of the judge's slippery tongue and dirty talk, she had seen a window of opportunity with Hugh but it had closed as fast as it had opened.

In the morning she told him that she always went to a café for breakfast; that she read the daily rag over a cappuccino. She didn't ask him to join her so he went his own way and ate a huge quantity of prunes, baked beans, tomatoes, bacon, eggs, fried bread, croissants, cereal, butter and jam in a coffee bar fairly near to where Lizzie was reading her newspaper.

After that he returned to Lincolnshire.

He was relieved to find that the playpen had disappeared and that no trace of Phyllis showed itself.

Melanie, during their listless lunch, had told him that she planned to spend some consecutive weeks in the cottage that she had bought on a whim in order to distance herself from her formidable social life in London.

He looked forward to having another crack at her. Seeing a bit of her. Every bit.

He changed into his country gear and thought of calling on Muriel or, failing that, on Marco and Flavia. He needed company; fidgety after his futile and truncated escapade with Lizzie in London. It was perhaps wiser not to call on Muriel for he remembered the danger of sighting Phyllis. He had not heard of her newfound employment with the judge. It was still very cold and he pulled out an extra jumper as he dithered over whether to target Marco and Flavia.

He noticed, as he sorted himself out, that there was a letter for him that had been delivered when he was away. It had come by airmail from South Africa. He unpacked his sponge bag – aperients, mouthwash, electric toothbrush – and arranged them like a little army, fighting for his life, beside the basin.

He opened the stiff envelope and sat down heavily as he read the typed sheet. It came from a solicitor and told him that he had fathered a little boy in South Africa. His eyes began to dance and to water but he had not even read the name of the declaring mother before his concentration fully left him. He did just manage to stand and allow his eyes to swivel to the looking-glass in front of which he preened and straightened his tie.

Pearl, perhaps, or Gloria. A beige brother for Marco. Uncle to Cleopatra. He and Muriel were still married and the little bundle might have a claim on Bradstow Manor. Anything, in his manliness, became possible.

When he was steadier he returned to the letter. Good God. They were soon to be on their way. Mother and child. Due to arrive within weeks and expecting to be met at the nearest station. The mother was neither Pearl nor Gloria but the estranged wife of a Belgian banker. Only once, too, he recalled dimly as the episode returned to irk him. The night he had arrived in Johannesburg. They had stayed at the same modest hotel and he had been disorientated – Muriel refusing to join him and missing his dog.

'Marcelle' had tracked him down somehow and the boy must be about the same age as Cleopatra. He was called Pierre. Peter. Too many Peters already.

A walk was the answer. Might do him good.

In the courtyard he was startled. Was that really Cleopatra in a peek-a-boo bonnet with a dummy, trailing a vast bow, in her mouth? It was, presumably, the old pram that she was strapped into but along the edges of the hood crawled felt mice in floral headgear carrying cocktail umbrellas. The carriage was painted mauve and the bar of the handle glistened with silver spray.

From under a grubby sleeve, cigarette smoke threaded and evaporated in the cold air. Tommy, who was wearing a very flat grey hat, beamed.

'Here's Grandad, my little lovely.' He pinched the baby's cheek and told Hugh that he had devoured a book on Norland nursing, 'potty training and the lot', and was now in full charge of Cleopatra.

'One has never felt so fulfilled.'

Hugh asked whether one might feel even more fulfilled if one had two, so to speak, to care for. The pram had been designed for two in the first place.

'Why not? Double trouble as they say. Double pennies too, please. One might get the creative urge and dress them to match.'

'It's a boy. Pierre. Peter.'

Tommy winked, 'I shall call him Pee-Pee. What's the difference so long as she's pretty.'

The dummy slithered from Cleopatra's mouth and she started to howl. It seemed she didn't like the notion of sharing her pram with a boy called Peter – especially if he was to be dressed as a girl. She didn't know, of course, that he would also be her uncle.

In the distance Hugh saw Muriel walking with Peter and Monopoly. Curtains were closed in the barn. It was already afternoon but still early for Marco and Flavia. He trudged alongside Tommy Tiddler whose stupefying scent drifted, intermingled with cigarette smoke, as strongly in the outdoor weather as ever it had done elsewhere.

Muriel, spotting him, was dismayed to see that Hugh had hurried back from London but said to Peter, 'So. That's that. Phyllis gone for good. Hugh, with a bit of luck, subdued and Cleopatra. Oh God.'

They watched the eccentric group move slowly as Tommy navigated the pram along a path, Hugh at his side.

For the time being, at least, Muriel planned, with the help of Peter, to reign over her kingdom comparatively undisturbed.

The following day Hugh took up with Melanie who had hastened to Lincolnshire in pursuit of him and who 'understood' everything. She elected to drive him to the station when the day came for him to meet with the estranged wife of the Belgian banker and the boy who, he had been assured, resembled him. Marcelle, the boy's mother, having handed over the baby, took the next train back to London. Hugh barely recognised her and they spoke few words to each other.

Hugh, fed up with the squash court, moved in with Melanie and they lived off the generous proceeds of the near-Bronzino. It had turned out to be a rare contemporary copy and Muriel gave it to him in exchange for a divorce.

Before long a large glass extension and another full story were added to Melanie's cottage. She was childless and declared herself 'over the moon' to take in little Pierre whose mother had returned to the Belgian banker on his condition that her aberration with Hugh in Johannesburg was never mentioned. Melanie also made the condition that Tommy Tiddler was to be fully employed to look after both Cleopatra and her small uncle.

Tommy, after dressing and spraying Cleopatra with scent each morning, took to fetching Pierre, popping him into the pram and spraying him behind the ears; that and around the rim of each peek-a-boo bonnet.

'Sneaked in a little mimosa sprinkler,' he mentioned to Hugh who walked down the path to greet the group as they set off for one of their morning outings.

'One of the tots might do a toilet and one doesn't want stinky-poo if one has to do a speedy changums, does one?'

Cleopatra and Pierre spent most of their time with Tommy at the Old School House where, in a newly-fashioned night-nursery, he had painted a mural. It consisted of several centaurs – each with their heads depicting various members of the community; Dawson in dog collar, Delilah with very curly hair, Alastair wearing a wistful smile; Dulcie, Muriel, Peter, Hugh, Melanie and others but none of them skilfully achieved and therefore unrecognisable. The dog collar gave a hint but that, too, was smudged – so no feelings had to be wounded.

Melanie, although perfectly happy to be a proxy parent, was also happy to enjoy Hugh's son and grand-daughter at a distance. She had no wish for them to cause any destruction in her newly rebuilt house – or to the thatched music room, also newly built, at the end of the garden.

Chapter 21

Hugh waved the unlikely cortège away with a coura-
geous smile and returned to Melanie who was percolat-
ing coffee in the well-appointed kitchen.

'This knife sharpener was a good buy, Melanie.' He sat
and delighted in his comfort and new purchases.

He had been practising riding a bicycle without using
the handlebars so as to be able to play the flageolet as he
peddled up the village street. It was a small, flute-like,
instrument with four finger holes on top and two thumb
holes below. He had found it in the attic at Bradstow
Manor. Muriel had seen no reason why he shouldn't take
that along with the near-Bronzino and various other
musical instruments, including sheet music. Mostly
glees and madrigals.

As he and Melanie set knives aside before embarking
on the adventure of turning the handle and achieving
sparkling results, he suggested, 'I think we ought to get
around to organising our madrigal evening. It's going to
take careful planning. Christening of the music room.
Local talent.'

'It's up to you, Hugh dear. I wonder who we'll ask.'

He kissed her with a long look and slightly swollen lips that had suffered from his bicycle rides, as he guided the wheels partly with his knees and partly with the pressure of his weight, with the flageolet in his mouth.

They had put finishing touches to the thatched music room. There was a platform set up with music stands and many uncomfortable chairs waited for an audience.

'We might kick off with "Dainty Fine Bird". Something like that.'

'I love the one about the swan, Hugh. You sing that so tunefully.' He smiled and stood up straight at the foot of the table, just beyond the knife sharpener and sang, 'The Dying Swan when Leeving had Noo Nooote.'

'Oh Hugh. I hope we can find some voices as lovely as yours. Of course, in London, I knew professionals – but here …'

Melanie's London friends had not attempted to bother her and she was without a circle. She ran round in them, though, gleeful at all she had gained.

Delilah, it turned out, had a strong voice, if sharp, and put herself forward as part of a quartet. The other two voices were also recruited locally and were a husband-and-wife team with some experience.

It rained on the day of the party although it had been planned for mid-June. Guests were allowed to leave umbrellas in the half-timbered porch and took to their uncomfortable seats in squelching shoes.

Dawson on his own (Delilah was performing and thus waiting excitedly behind the scenes), Muriel and Peter. The judge and Phyllis, Tommy with a child on each knee, even Dulcie, as well as many others, sat there as Hugh, on tiptoe and eyes turned to heaven, gave short explanations before each 'piece'.

Melanie acted wanly as a modest but knowing hostess wearing a bemused and self-deprecating smile as she mumbled, 'Very local, I'm afraid. Not like a London "do" at all, but very touching.'

Marco and Flavia were not there. With the newfound freedom made possible by Tommy Tiddler, they spent little time in their barn, escaping to London where they had the full use of Muriel's house. Thanks to the good Bronzino copy, Hugh had no further need for the rent.

Muriel wallowed in the comparative peace and Delilah pronounced the whole set-up as 'modern but, aren't we all God's creatures?'

Chapter 22

Marco and Flavia were in the West Indies. Roger had managed to wangle a freebie for them from some newspaper, hoping that he might at some stage get Moggan to spill the beans if a royal connection could be made. Peter suggested to Muriel that they ask Hugh and Melanie to lunch.

She rang their number and Melanie answered, saying, 'What a nice gesture.'

Muriel was counting the stitches of her knitting when they arrived. She was working a pullover for Peter in cable stitch. The texture of the surface was planned so that he would finger and feel the work and know how she had striven to perfect it. It was a complicated pattern and involved safety pins. She had become addicted to knitting. It soothed her and it reminded Peter of his early experiences with twigs and string. Whatever the drawbacks of daily life, whatever the unwelcome interruptions, knitting grew and went forward – however slowly. Something to return to. A target, a row to be finished – an achievement. It was maddening to be stalled.

Muriel had become more and more observant

– studying the skill in order to describe all she saw to Peter.

Melanie was tall and thin and wore very gloomy, expensive, dark brown and grey clothes. Funny little flat shoes and no jewellery. The overall effect was, Muriel considered, extremely turgid. The accent was on pure wool and raw silk. She looked both pure and raw as she spoke very softly with her head bent downwards.

'You must be the first to know. Hugh and I are planning to commit matrimony.'

Hugh looked quite pleased with himself as she went on. 'I think I can boast that I've tamed him somewhat. It must be said that he has tamed me too. I used to live a very different life in London.'

She looked to the floor before starting again. 'Mostly showbiz people and writers of course. I haven't invited them here yet. I don't feel the good life would suit them. They are loyal, though, and several have sent kind messages in reply to our change of address card.'

The telephone rang and Muriel answered it in some irritation. It was Mambles who rushed straight in, 'Mummy wants to know if we can visit. She's been depressed – the young ones are stealing all the thunder and that frightful fancy footman is giving her too many Martinis – making her fractious.'

'Yes. Soon. I'm busy now, Mambles, but I'll ring you this evening.'

'Why are you always busy? Who have you got with you? Tell them it's me.'

'I'm sorry but I can't talk now.'

'Mummy says she hopes we don't have to see that wan widow, if that's what she is, who's taken up with your former.'

Princess Matilda never, ever used the word 'husband'.

On she went – coming near to pleading with Muriel to hear of Cunty's need for a pacemaker and Moggan's prostate operation but Muriel gabbled and rang off as Peter offered the guests something to drink and as Hugh said, 'Melanie doesn't but I'm ready for refreshment.'

At lunch Muriel encouraged Melanie to do the talking. It helped to sidestep plaintive remarks from Hugh and amused Peter.

She said, 'That Tommy Tiddler is straight from heaven. I don't allow him to smoke under my roof so the children spend most of their time at the School House where he gives them cooking demonstrations. He calls them the little darlings and wears a chef's hat with a Peter Pan motif pinned on it.'

Hugh looked around for a sign of Monopoly who sulked upstairs.

Melanie, part confident, part unsure, tried to reach a degree of affinity with Muriel as the brothers talked of music.

She spoke with exasperating softness, watery and rhetorical. 'Delilah is a character, isn't she? Kitty is sweet, isn't she? Tommy's a card, isn't he?'

Was she being deferential? Proving she knew as much if not more? Was Muriel not allowed to imagine that she was a hop ahead? She was mystified. Baffled by the spurious bid for intimacy.

'Funny. You and me, Muriel. Married to brothers – sisters-in-law in a way.' Funny way, Muriel thought. I'm not married to Peter and was married to Hugh until a few months ago – until I parted with enough money to allow him to set up house with you.

Melanie went on and on. 'I know Hugh played you up but, as I said, we have tamed each other.'

As they left she said, 'Of course I do miss my showbiz friends. I wish I could ask them here but, unless of course you had royalty staying – royals combine well with them, don't you think? Keep me and Hugh posted. We may be a respectable married couple by then.'

Muriel didn't know what to think. She'd had her fill of politicians and was weary of Queens and Princesses. 'Gosh, yes. Not for a bit, I hope.'

She yearned to get back to her forty-fourth row and worried that she was getting short of wool – planning to write and order more as soon as Hugh and Melanie left. As they did so a nasty glint came into Melanie's eye. A touch of malice showed even though her voice was soft and timid. 'It's easy for you to entertain in style here. You're very fortunate. I'll get Tommy to do us some starters but it would be a help to have good advance warning.'

Chapter 23

Mambles had wangled another visit with Mummy in the spring. In the past the two had travelled together to the north of Scotland but, with ever increasing shadows of anility crossing each face, long journeys had become a thing of the past.

'Just for two nights,' Mambles had pleaded, 'we'll bring Cunty and Farty, and Moggan is free to drive us.'

Everything fell into place. Same rooms, same accessories provided and, with a few variations, the same conversations.

Muriel invited Hugh and Melanie to lunch although Mambles had no wish to see him in the company of his wan new companion.

Melanie curtseyed before the Queen Mother and half-whispered, 'Normally, as a new bride, I enter the room first but today I am honoured to take second place when we proceed to the dining room.'

The old lady said that she had once been a bride herself – at Westminster Abbey.

Hugh, although still smarting after the donkey debacle

since, on that day, he had assumed the role of group leader, suggested that, after lunch, he take Her Majesty to look at the garden which was alive with spring flowers.

They set off gingerly. Hugh held her by one of her arms. Her free hand clasped a stick with an ivory handle that had some sort of royal crest engraved on it. Cunty followed.

He saw to his consternation that a crow-trap had been set up in grass that had just begun to shoot up high. It was a large netted contraption with a bar across it from which a dead rabbit swung – held up by two rotting legs. Inside the trap three crows, jammed together, fluttered and twisted – frantic to be free. At his charge's insistence Hugh told her what he saw – playing down the extent of the horror of the bird's suffering. 'That,' she replied, 'will be a Larsen trap. We have them on the grouse moor at my castle in Scotland. We hang up their carcasses to keep the raptors at bay. They are, as you must know, short-distance migrants and very territorial.'

Muriel, faintly anxious, joined them and as she looked at Hugh in his near-awkwardness clinging to the buoyant old lady's arm, she remembered how handsome he had been and how he had fooled her. Confident. Go-ahead. It had not hit her then that he was merely conceited. She wondered if, even in the early days, he had suspected her of having 'connections'.

After the little party set out she had worried that Hugh in his defiantly worn clothes might test his masculinity even on a nonagenarian. The expression 'anything in a skirt' came to her and this particular nonagenarian was presumably wearing a skirt under a tight-fitting black coat. Muriel was shaken by the sight of the Larsen trap. Her mother had often told her that she would never be a proper country person. Her constantly puzzled mind shook about with images of mediaeval tortures. Punishment in stocks. She hoped it was just a dark patch that she passed through. She was trying to knit a doll for Cleopatra but had no idea where to buy the right ingredients to stuff it with.

With heaving and sighing, Dulcie was beside them. 'That's where some of your bloody visitors should be. Fighting for their lives in a cage.'

Chapter 24

Summer came and went and the gap on the wall – left by the Bronzino in the front hall – had been camouflaged by skilled re-hanging of pictures.

Hugh, having moved in with Melanie, had left the squash court empty and Flavia decided to start a business there. She called it Stretchable Chic and busied herself collecting together as many elasticated garments as were traceable. Boob tubes, girdles, tights, saucy garters, and every sort of tensile knicker. She had written to Ann Summers asking her to come to Lincolnshire to open the affair in a stretch limo but had not, by autumn, had a reply.

Muriel tidied most of Flavia's risqué merchandise away onto the gallery where the futon had lived during Hugh's occupation of the squash court and planned to pull her weight in the neighbourhood. After discussions with Delilah it was decided that a musical evening in aid of the church tower was to be the answer. Hugh's had not been for the church but simply a social affair and those he considered humble villagers had been excluded.

He was pained, though, by Muriel's decision and told Melanie, woefully, that she had never had ideas of her own – always been guided by him. Nonetheless he was prepared to contribute to the success of her evening.

An upright piano from the loft was moved across the yard and Peter was made to promise to play for performers when the day came.

Hugh asked if he might play some unaccompanied Bach on the flute. Perhaps Debussy too.

Sonia, who warbled, wished to be allowed to sing 'All I want is a Room Somewhere' and 'The Song of the Kerrie Dancers' provided that she be given many hours of practice – with Peter at the piano beforehand. Eric, deserting his crossness always displayed in the garden, suggested he should play on his piano accordion 'Knees up Mother Brown and Speed Bonnie Boat'.

The head teacher planned to read from the children's homework and Tommy Tiddler wrote to say that he was preparing to do his imitation of the Queen Mother unless she was to be there in person in which case he was happy to alter the programme and impersonate Mrs Thatcher.

Judge Jack sent a special messenger in the shape of Phyllis, who now drove him everywhere in his old Mercedes, to deliver a letter. 'Hail to my neighbour! You may not know what talent I hide under my bushel. I am more than happy to help you with your musical evening – anything to support the church. In times gone by, in Sandra's day when the boys were young, I used to do my own rendering of 'Danny Boy' after the Queen's speech on Christmas Day. Phyllis (what a treasured find, dear lady) will be at the wheel in case I take a little something for Dutch courage before taking to the stage.'

Marco volunteered to be master of ceremonies and Lizzie invited herself to stay: 'I'll be a tremendous help. Hand sandwiches round and make conversation. I hope that awful judge won't be there with that ex-housekeeper of yours.'

Chapter 25

Muriel drowned in a whirligig of time, motion and noise – her head nibbled at by a series of different sounds. The much-planned evening had taken place and she walked home, across the yard, with Peter and Monopoly.

It was all still there – nibbling at her head.

Sonia, accompanied by Peter, standing on tiptoe, eyes raised as she carolled harshly 'Oh! For one of those hours of madness ...' as if she had need to summon a single second of her own insanity.

Hugh, throat cleared and face set as he fingered his flute ready to perform an unaccompanied piece by Debussy. Hitherto, Muriel had believed that it was impossible to play a flute badly but Hugh's performance, possibly due to his fingers being on the fat side, put paid to that belief as he inhaled air from the crowded room where patient parishioners sat to listen with curiosity. Marco, starting to sway, mouthing the words, 'Good blow job, Pa.'

Judge Jack, tipsy and gazed at by Phyllis who had, earlier, found a drawer filled with his dead wife's trinkets – all of which she wore – singing 'Danny Boy' with tuneless gusto. Marco, a lively conductor, introducing the head teacher who held a huge collection of children's exercise books from which she read extracts.

Performance after performance.

Lizzie searching for gratitude each time she passed the Twiglets round.

Flavia, dressed from top to toe in sequinned rubber, distributing pamphlets that told of Stretchable Chic and future exhibits.

By far the most popular act, though, was Tommy Tiddler's impersonation of the Queen Mother (he had found a friend from the pub to look after Cleopatra and Pee-Pee for the evening) – although some did not know where to look.

He made a dramatic entry from behind an improvised curtain and was draped in a patchwork quilt of many pale colours.

It was held together on one shoulder by a gold brooch engraved with two lesbians engaged in something oral. His hair was powdered white and held in a net. Face powdered too and a sweet, gracious smile sat engraved on his lips. He walked slowly and majestically waving one hand stiffly and turning his head from side to side so as to give pleasure to each person in the audience.

Clapping. Cheering. Delilah, doubtful about the lack of reverence for royalty but grateful for the ticket money that helped rebuild the church tower.

Muriel, drowning still, but a part, at last, of the community, the church and of village life.

Courtyard crossed, she went to bed with Peter who whispered, 'Brilliant. Let's do it every year.'

ALSO BY SUSANNA JOHNSTON

Muriel Pulls It Off

Muriel Pulls It Off is a comic romp about a mid-fifty-year-old woman who, having been rather lost in her London life, suddenly and out of the blue inherits a marvellous Elizabethan manor house in Lincolnshire from a lunatic old man to whom she is vaguely related.

Muriel goes to live there but is constantly dogged by her London friends : feckless son and daughter-in-law, old drunk lover, a pretender to the inheritance and Princess Matilda – youngest and invented daughter of George VI and the Queen Mother – who insists on bringing 'Mummy' and other bits of Greek royalty with her. Our heroine has huge difficulty fitting this in with ghastly old retainers, and the local vicar and his wife Delilah. She is also lumbered with her ex-husband's dog – which she dislikes – and is in love with her ex-husband's brother, who is blind. Her ex-husband turns up to share in the spoils when he hears of her inheritance (he is a disgraced MP). There's also Miss Crunthard, ex-royal governess. The royal family had a penchant for the dishing out of nicknames and King George VI was unable to pronounce his 'r's – thus she is always known as 'Cunty'. Royals didn't see anyting wrong but courtiers found it embarrassing. However, all ends happily thanks to Princess Matilda's rank.

'Susanna is the mistress of what the Surrealists called "Black Humour", the queen of deliberate outrage and offensive scandal. Here, she is in top mischievous form. Her characters, real or invented, most often both, will limp out of the pages bleeding, maimed and furious' GEORGE MELLY

ISBN : 1-905147-24-4

EDITED BY SUSANNA JOHNSTON

Late Youth
An Anthology Celebrating the Joys of Being Over Fifty

Grey is the new black – old is the new young.

Contributors:
Anthony Blond, Arabella Boxer, Melvyn Bragg, Georgia Campbell, Alexander Chancellor, George Christie, Maureen Cleave, Isabel Colegate, Jilly Cooper, Polly Devlin, Deborah Devonshire, Lindy Dufferin, Dame Edna Everage, Julian Fane, Desmond Fitzgerald, Christopher Gibbs, Colin Glenconner, Jonathan Guinness, Maggi Hambling, Selina Hastings, Drue Heinz, Min Hogg, Hugh Honour, Elizabeth Jane Howard, Angela Huth, Francis King, Lucinda Lambton, Kenneth Jay Lane, Patrick Leigh Fermor, Anthony Little, Roddy Llewellyn, Rupert Loewenstein, Candida Lycett Green, Deborah MacMillan, George Melly, John Julius Norwich, David Plante, Jeffrey Smart, John Stefanidis, David Tang, Teresa Waugh, Natalie Wheen, Peregrine Worsthorne – and many more.

'Light, gossipy, upbeat. Based on a well-heeled, well-connected circle of friends and relations … good, stout-hearted stuff, in aid of a good cause' **ANNE CHISHOLM**, *Spectator*

'I never think about age, which is probably why I have remained spookily youthful. I stay young because I pick up the Gift of Life and run with it – in heels' **DAME EDNA EVERAGE**

ISBN: 1-905147-09-0